THE
PERP
WALK

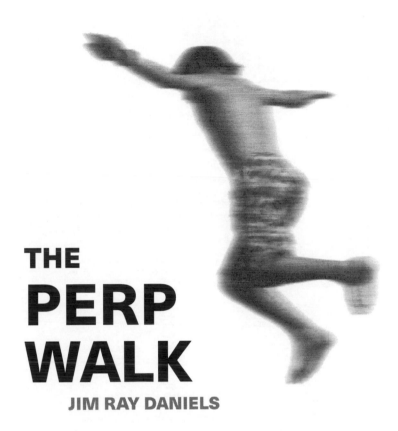

THE
PERP
WALK

JIM RAY DANIELS

Michigan State University Press | *East Lansing*

♾ The paper used in this publication meets the minimum requirements
of ANSI/NISO Z39.48-1992 (R 1997) (Permanence of Paper).

Michigan State University Press
East Lansing, Michigan 48823-5245

The Perp Walk is a work of fiction. All incidents, dialogue, and characters
are products of the author's imagination and are not to be construed as real.
Any resemblance to persons living or dead is entirely coincidental.

Printed and bound in the United States of America.

28 27 26 25 24 23 22 21 20 19   1 2 3 4 5 6 7 8 9 10

LIBRARY OF CONGRESS CATALOGING-IN-PUBLICATION DATA
Names: Daniels, Jim, 1956– author.
Title: The perp walk / Jim Ray Daniels.
Description: East Lansing : Michigan State University Press, [2019]
Identifiers: LCCN 2018035318| ISBN 9781611863161 (pbk. : alk. paper)
| ISBN 9781609175955 (pdf) | ISBN 9781628953619 (epub) | ISBN 9781628963625 (kindle)
Classification: LCC PS3554.A5635 A6 2019 | DDC 813/.54—dc23
LC record available at https://lccn.loc.gov/2018035318

Book design by Charlie Sharp, Sharp Designs, East Lansing, MI
Cover design by Shaun Allshouse, www.shaunallshouse.com
Cover art is *absprung*, by Klaus Epee, and is used under license from Adobe Stock.

Michigan State University Press is a member of the Green Press Initiative and is
committed to developing and encouraging ecologically responsible publishing
practices. For more information about the Green Press Initiative and the use of
recycled paper in book publishing, please visit *www.greenpressinitiative.org*.

Visit Michigan State University Press at *www.msupress.org*

CONTENTS

Circling Squares

B rick-box houses. *Boom.* One, then another. Car-clunk over concrete rectangles of street divided by tar spacers. Trip over cracked sidewalk squares lined with weeds to the front door. *Boom.* Slabs. No dreaming here, baby. No hidden jewels. Just red brick, orange. Blank dominoes not falling. Already played. Four walls. *Boom.* Streets not plowed nor salted—not in the budget. Snow rutted by bald tires. Ice crust. Bumper-hitch for kicks. Detroit and Warren side-swiping each other daily on Eight Mile Road. *Boom.* Cost of doing business. Boot hockey. Broken Nose/Fat Lip/Black Eye/Red Slush—street names. Signs of love to keep bodies warm, mark territory. *Boom.* Stop. Too late. Nostalgia for blood! *Boom.* Drive slow. Nobody behind you. Lost yet? No. Yes. No payoff in breaking in. We're the ones breaking in—further from the city: bigger houses, bigger yards, more cover. More doors, windows. More stuff. Blood for its own sake. Sighs of affection. Signs of infection. No *Vote For* signs. No *For Sale* signs. *For Sale* sighs. What they asking? 50s tract housing. Stuck zipper of the assembly line. *Boom.*

Kids. *Boom. Boom. Boom.* Who's giving in/up? *Against* signs. Cruising for a bruising. Will the old names drift off in bitter wind, ripped from identical mailboxes? Nobody changing up houses crammed onto cloned lots. *Boom.* Tour guide. Engine. Caboose. Cranky crossing guard with a heart of bile. Hi, Hi, Hi, Hi. Bye, bye, bye, bye. You got a vein like that? Insider on the outside. Roll down the window. The old curses swarm. Old names flattened into a litany of slabs. Rectangles and squares. Rotary-dialed phone numbers of the dead. Graffiti prayer. We used to. We don't anymore. We roamed streets copying house numbers on torn sheets of loose leaf. Our streets. For comfort. *Boom.* Nothing to loosen. Nothing to lose. Cement streets crack, crumble. Not in the budget. *See ya. Wouldn't wanna be ya.* But I am am am ya. *Boom.* Why stop, why yield? Why idle? New dogs tricked with the same barks sniff each other's butts at the fence line. *Boom.* No bite. The butts of all our jokes forever.

They Swim

"My mom and dad don't fuck!" Sliver said. Sliver—he hated the nickname, so it stuck. We stood gathered in the weedy field behind Bronco Lanes off of Eight Mile and Ryan where we'd carved out an asymmetrical baseball diamond in the weeds—to get from second to third required good wind, and we'd started to smoke, so we hit a lot of doubles.

It had come up—fucking—and Sliver had jumped in without thinking. His father was a deacon at their church, his mother obese and foul-mouthed. If I hadn't read about it in the slim pamphlet my mother slipped me years earlier—something she picked up at the doctor's office where she worked as a receptionist—I might've thought he had a point.

Sliver—short, scrawny, baby-faced, slow, shy—an easy target for our snowballs, slingshots, peashooters—the relentless cruelty we relied on, thinking it made us cool. Didn't every cluster of friends in every neighborhood have one, the butt of, the Sliver of all jokes?

———————

So much I don't recall, but I remember Queen Anne's lace and milkweed, the stagnant, humid smell in that field in summer heat before we had paper routes or jobs, when we had all the time in the world to sharpen our sticks, to try out swear words in our mouths like a new spicy communion host, like some adult religion we weren't supposed to know about or participate in. Like prayers our parents had memorized for secret adult services we weren't invited to, a language we were supposed to ignore.

I can tell you who was there, I can sing the innocent names of our freckled, gap-toothed faces—or maybe we already had our adult teeth? At least some of them. No one was named Opie. Our fathers steered clear of sheriffs and their deputies.

———————

We might've looked like some cute-movie kids or a B group of Little Rascals, but we were too big for our britches. We wanted to burn our britches but were still figuring out what that meant, what we might wear in our next lives as teenagers—all of us except Angelo, an older boy of some undetermined age who was not quite right. Was not right at all, so *not* right that we could tease him without hurting his feelings, which was no fun, so we quickly turned to Sliver instead. We protected Angelo, included him for many years in all of our summer games. He went to a special school on a special bus.

"What do you mean, they don't fuck?" I said. "Of course they fuck."

"How do you know?" Sliver looked around at the rest of us with those wide eyes of sincere wonder the girls would come to love. His older brother Gene slunk off into the weeds to hit stones with his bat.

All of our bats were from Free Bat Day at Tiger Stadium. In fact, Sliver's stepfather Paul—Gene's dad—had arranged the excursion, gotten us tickets donated by his church. At the time, we did not know we were Underprivileged Youth.

"They swim," Miss Bohinski said, red flaring up her high cheeks like in an ancient cartoon. We all had secret crushes on her. How do I know, if they were secret? She was the only young, single female teacher at St. Mike's who was not a nun. Not everybody would've labeled it a crush, but we acted weird in her classes, either listening to the angel on one shoulder or the devil on the other, instead of ignoring them both and being our normal selves. The girls noticed, and their own angels and devils responded. Miss Bohinski—we learned her first name was Brandi, and we didn't know anyone who had an i in place of the standard y—in retrospect, probably had an eating disorder. Her thinness—severe, alarming, alluring—made her look younger, and she was already younger, so in our imaginations, she almost looked like one of us. Was there a Saint Brandi?

They swim. But we could not. Our sperm could swim to the egg and make a scandal, a disaster, a disappearance, a premature wedding, a black eye, and, in one sad case, a murder at a wedding. Oh, they were all sad cases, weren't they, Rita?

My friend Rita and I have a kid out there somewhere who must be grown now. Me, the one who knew how it all worked, who mocked Sliver. Kid must be twenty-three. Perhaps already experiencing male-pattern baldness and a sensitivity to latex. What did they name him? *Him.* We knew it was a boy. *They* who adopted him.

"Are they fucking now, Sliver?"

"If you run home, maybe you'll catch them."

"The Immaculate Conception of Sliver."

"Ever seen a stork, you dork?"

Gene had disappeared entirely, so the game was called off due to imbalanced hormones and teams.

———————————

They swim. And we had no place to learn how, crowded by cement and filth, enormous factories and stifling box houses. You can't swim in a sprinkler, and we'd outgrown those sweet water-dances of childhood. We preferred sweating and swearing. Somebody must have learned how to—it doesn't make sense that a whole neighborhood couldn't swim. Once we were old enough to learn to drive, Brad, Rita's older half-brother (we were full of halfs and steps—even now I get them confused), got a transportation special that his father had fixed up in the alley behind their house and sold to him for $100. A Plymouth Fury. We piled in the car, and Brad drove us out to Metro Beach on Lake St. Clair, squeezed in without seatbelts. At least seven of us. The kind of ride that seemed to end up in the newspapers: Teenagers killed in single-car crash on straight road. We'd all learn firsthand about that when he drove a carload into a ditch on Outer Drive, killing some lonely, clueless freshman who'd hopped in the car for his first and last joy ride.

We wore our cutoff jeans for the trip, scissored crooked above the blown-out worn-out knees. We usually wore our long jeans and suffered. You could take your shirt off, but wearing shorts was wimpy. T-shirt, jeans, tube socks, sneakers. Sneers.

I could write a book on my neighborhood—or maybe more of a pamphlet, like the one my mother gave me about sex—to explain how things worked there, things that seem ridiculous, but were our facts of life.

We ran down to the beach with its sludgy, trucked-in sand, suspiciously muddy between our toes. We walked in up to our waists and splashed water off our white, white bellies, shouting out odd barking noises, intoxicated by how they carried in that open space over water. All good until a group of three girls who had been eyeing us got up off their towels—all Mickey Mouse towels, which seemed weird to me, like they were in some cult, though I'm sure we also looked like we were in a cult with our matching cutoffs and truckers' tans.

The girls splashed through the water next to us and swam out to the wooden raft anchored in the roped-off swim zone. One of them laughed as she climbed out of the water onto the rocking deck floating on empty oil barrels. She saw me staring and waved, shouting, "Come out and join us!" She gave me a wet, brilliant smile. They wore string bikinis, not the modest kind our sisters wore. Pale flesh threatening to be revealed by a loose knot. Our shoes randomly untied themselves, so why not bikinis? They were our age, or older—maybe even college students. Metro Beach, the closest one to Warren, was about twenty miles away from Eight Mile Road. Anything was possible out there where nobody knew what jerks we were.

After she yelled again, "C'mon you guys, join us!" the other guys noticed.

I can't say what the distance was, though it did not matter, the water out there clearly over our heads. Despite knowing that *they swim*, we knew we could not. Gene began wading toward them, all the way up to his neck. He briefly lost his footing and slipped under, then frantically splashed his way back into the shallows where we waited. We burned quickly in that sun.

Our high school, Eight Mile—we called it Hate Smiles, the best nickname we could come up with (sorry, Sliver, we should have done better by you too)—had a swimming pool, but it was closed for future repairs all four years I attended. Our parents had voted down a millage increase to fix the pool and turn the football field from cinders to grass. Wait—did we really play on cinders? It wasn't grass. Mostly dirt and weeds—they put something in it to keep the mud down.

We broke into the school once. That's how sick we were. Probably drunk. Often, we'd end up in the school parking lot on weekend nights.

Cars full of teenagers waiting for other cars to pull up. We'd roll down our windows and say, "Hey, what's up?" And "Where's the party?" We were always looking for a party, but there was no party. Or, we weren't invited. Or, if there was a party, it lasted thirty seconds before the police arrived to break it up.

The Warren Police Department seemed to consist of Vietnam veterans or angry punks too young or too old for Vietnam but angry nevertheless. When not harassing black youths who mistakenly wandered across Eight Mile Road from Detroit, they contented themselves with harassing local white teenagers.

We contented ourselves with the knowledge that at least we weren't black and thus were far less likely to get thunked on the head by one of those giant flashlights. Detroit had their police helicopters, so Warren got a couple old ones donated by the Army. One of the pilots, a vet, bought his booze in Max's, the party store I worked at during high school. The way his fingers danced on the counter waiting for me to pull down his bottle of Kessler's, I could imagine him pulling the trigger on a helicopter machine gun, mowing us down on concrete streets. The helicopters were underutilized and eventually mothballed. All they could do was hover and spray their searchlight down on our parties until the landlocked cop cars arrived.

———————

Sliver left us while we were in high school. When I think of it these years later, I'm still shocked by stone-cold fear hollowing out my insides to create an ice cave of shame and cowardice.

Vietnam hovered like helicopters above those pockmarked streets. Some of us got beamed up and never returned. Some of us were too young. Some of us were named Angelo and never went anywhere. The local juvie judge was notorious for offering the choice of either incarceration or military service. When somebody got busted, we knew they'd be getting that buzz cut pronto—everyone chose the Army. We were amateur soldiers who got along to get along, who never admitted fear yet felt it constantly. We could not make a baseball diamond with ninety-foot bases or swim.

We climbed up a thick, black, ropy wire stapled up the side of the school all the way to the roof. We did not get electrocuted. We found a hatch open and climbed down. We shot baskets in the gym. We made announcements over the PA system. Someone threw up on the principal's desk—I'm not saying who. We weren't sure how much trouble we wanted to get into. We sobered up. We climbed down the ladder into the empty swimming pool, a big crack in it where cement had shifted.

The diving board had been removed. We walked down the slope into the deep end. We moved our arms in swimming motions. We puffed our cheeks out and held our breath. We smoked waterproof cigarettes. We played Marco Polo, a game explained to us by Oscar, who had cousins in Sterling Heights with a backyard pool. Drunk on the echo of our own voices off tile: *Marco! Polo! Marco! Polo!* we shouted, long after the game was over. I still don't know who Marco Polo was, and don't bother telling me.

They swim. Life begins to turn with two words in a fifth grade classroom. Were we really that old? That young?

Within eight years, most of us were working in the auto plants—not just the guys either. Some of the Future Homemakers of America joined the Future Shoprats of America, and we warily coexisted—with each other, and with the blacks who crossed Eight Mile every day to punch in with the rest of us at the Chrysler plant at Eight Mile and Mound.

If we were swimming, we were inside a tiny fish tank, butting our noses against the glass while kids on a field trip pointed at us and laughed, not a clue to their own futures, despite the mirror we were offering.

If we were swimming, who was sprinkling the little food flakes on top? Who was tapping at the glass, shouting at us to get busy?

How many of us escaped? How many of us drowned? This is where my metaphors break down, where I join Angelo in inarticulate limbo. Even now, I am walking down the streets of the old neighborhood, limping like he did. Limping and singing sailor songs taught to me by those who walk on water. Escaping a fish tank is perhaps the most temporary of escapes—shorter than even those botched prison breaks I read about in the paper that seem concocted by felons who watched too many bad Hollywood movies.

You might be thinking Sliver—Steve, Stephen, that's his real name—died for his country in Vietnam at this point, but the shame is that he died for an even less clear and purposeful reason. It doesn't do justice to Denny Smolinski to say he was a bully. He was mean from day one, and thus sent to Vietnam by our juvie judge. The mystery for me is, why did he come back to school after two years away? I ripped out a sheet of looseleaf paper from my spiral notebook and gave it to him to take a test in the required American Government class, then gave him my answers to boot, glad that some of them were right.

He was so vicious that I ran from his smart and pretty sister who literally threw herself at me one night at a helicopter party. In the high school parking lot behind auto shop one day, Smolinski called out Sliver's stepdad who the night before had tried to scrub some racist graffiti off the wall, then decided it wasn't right for Sliver to not fight back, defend his family, so he—oh man, I stood frozen—stomped on Sliver's—Steve's— face with his thick black boots, metal horseshoe cleats hammered into the bottoms. We scattered and ran—some of us back into the school to rouse the security guards at either end of the long hallway. Some of us just kept on running.

Angelo wore a metal brace on one leg and limped when he walked. He referred to himself in the third person like a star athlete:

"Angelo has to go bathroom."

"Angelo happy. Angelo good."

The last day we played with him, he said "Angelo mad" and swung the bat at Gene, chasing him around the field. Lucky the brace slowed him down. We convinced him he was more valuable retrieving foul balls, and while he seemed to accept that, he soon stopped showing up altogether.

How slow was Angelo? He used to pick up dog shit from his yard and throw it over the fence into the field, but only after it had time to harden, so that's a slow somewhere between using a shovel and trying to pick up the soft stuff.

Our good-luck charm, he marched up and down Jackson and Ashville streets chanting loud Navy songs his father must have taught him, lifting and swinging the anchor of his bum leg like a metronome. Seeing Angelo meant someone was worse off than us, and maybe that's why we were kind to him. We knew whatever his future held after his parents died wasn't good. They were older than our parents. Maybe they'd adopted him. They never spoke to us. The only word we ever heard from them was "Angelo!" when they coaxed him home from the field. He was not allowed anywhere besides Jackson and Ashville streets and the field behind them that held our flawed diamond. "Sonny stay home," he'd say when we headed over to Archangel Street to shoplift at the little strip mall where the Bel-Air Theater used to be, on our side of Eight Mile.

I liked to rub Angelo's buzz cut like he was a favorite pet. He had the enormous smile of the damaged. I don't think the rest of us—our mouths didn't work like that.

"How do the sperms get to the eggs?" Sliver Wrobleski asked.

Miss Bohinski had been explaining reproduction with full-color flip charts in front of the room—all zoom on organs with no human figures. I was sure by the flush in her face that she was thinking of how the sperm got to the egg. A man and a woman. The transfer. Did some of us giggle into our hands? Or did we just squirm in silence? Whatever—that silence lasted a long time. Brandi looked at the clock for help, but we still had five minutes till the bell rang. Or was it Brandee? No y, in any case. She wore short skirts and clonked around on urgent high heels like a girl playing dress up. Those skirts hung around her waist like torn confessional curtains. We could see her bra straps, but she was more flat chested than some of the girls in our class. Remember, Rita?

But Brandi was not moving. The red transferred from her face to Sliver's and back like some mad contagion.

"Well, they swim, of course," Miss Bohinski finally sputtered, and though Steve raised his hand for a follow-up, frowning, motionless, Brandi flipped the charts back to the front page and began erasing a board that had no writing on it until the bell did, mercifully, ring.

They swim. The correct answer on the invisible final question on the exam. You had to guess the question, then write your answer.

"Your parents—all of our parents—they know how to swim," I explained to Stevie. And I made the circle with my thumb and index finger with one hand and took my other index finger and ran it back and forth inside that circle in the universal symbol for fucking.

"Swim like that," I added.

"The Fuck Stroke," Sliver added, seeking redemption, and he got it as we all sprawled laughing in the scratchy weeds.

Sliver's stepfather Paul—a mailman in better shape than our factory fathers from all that walking—seemed to have more time to think about being a dad. He got the Sunday School bus to take us to Bat Day. We each picked a different model from the rack near the admissions gates so that we'd have a variety to choose from in our pickup games in the field.

Paul came out one evening when we gathered in a clattered mass of bikes on the street to tell us not to call him Sliver anymore. "His name is Stephen. Steve. Got it?"

"Do you know how to swim?" somebody asked, maybe me.

───────────

I don't even want to tell you about the Showdown Game with the kids from Oscar's cousin's neighborhood.

I still don't quite understand real estate, but in the Detroit suburbs, the further from the city you were, the nicer the houses, and Sterling Heights was nicer than Warren in every way. Their swimming pool held water.

When Oscar's cousin was visiting from the "Heights"—as flat as Warren, maybe flatter—and played ball with us, he said, "The guys in my neighborhood would *kick* your guys' *asses*." We were beginning to understand the disdain of verbal italics. The challenge was made. "We'll bring our own bats," he said. "And a decent ball." We used an old mushed-up thing covered in black electrical tape. We'd grown to prefer it. Easier to find in the weeds. Tape seemed more natural to us than cowhide and stitching.

If this was a movie, the gritty kids from the other side of the tracks would triumph. I've found that most people who are successful claim to be from the other side of the tracks when they actually have no idea even where the tracks are to begin with. And if I have an underprivileged chimp on my shoulder, you better not try to knock it off. Chimps are always portrayed as harmless, but don't be fooled. Okay, we did get our asses kicked—you don't need a damn play-by-play, do you? And we didn't fare too well in the brawl at the end either.

And maybe it comes together here, and maybe not, but I'm thinking it was like learning that our parents did indeed fuck. Who knows when, but they did. A slight shift of the flat ground, and no one wanted to mention the embarrassing earthquake, imaginary and sensitive. No one ever cut the weeds in our field, but if they did, maybe we would've had our futures revealed a bit more clearly. Maybe we could've gone into it with a bit more dignity. The brawl wasn't with the kids from the Heights. As they packed up their gear in a nice canvas bag and loaded up their bikes, we tore into each other with blame, then fists.

Shell to the Ear

D *amn it.* A wrench clanks against cement from under a car up on blocks in the street. Lawn mower/leaf blower/snow blower taking care of business—the force of a fire hose to lick a stamp. If it doesn't spew and roar, it ain't working. We got special mufflers that make your car louder! Shhhh. An old woman unwraps a lozenge and crosses the street against idling traffic. The last pedestrian on earth. At least on Eight Mile Road. Perhaps lost, in search of the old country where walking was allowed, even encouraged. Calibrate your ears to barking dogs. Sick crunch of metal on metal. Tow truck beeping/backing up. Chain rattle. Trunk slam. Gate clink. Chain-link twang. Engine idle. Chug. Siren. Cough. Rev. Hi-lo in the machine-shop bay. Air hose. School bell. Lighter flick. Fast-food bag-rattle. Spit on the drive-thru hip-hop rock throb and buzz through open/closed windows. Lips kiss cigarettes outside AA meetings at old St. Mike's. Chopper bray. House-door: slam. Car-door: slam. Bar-door: slam. Alarm. Accident. Alarm. Gunshot. Don't pretend or imagine a backfire. Not here. Not now. Siren. Siren call. Folded in night's dark envelope. Flattened by fear/suspicion. Squeezed into wallets sweating in back pockets. Night train unloads parts at Chrysler Assembly. Metallic hiss-stream of traffic past Eight Mile High. Constant sea. Wave crash. Close your eyes or you won't hear it.

Quality of Light

We stood on the corner of Jackson and Ashville under the buzz and flicker of the stubborn dying streetlight—I wanted to put it out of its misery, but I had no gun and could not reach the sky. Misery. Does it really love company?

Gene leaned into Rita, her back arched against the rough, splintered wood of the streetlight pole while I mostly looked the other way, down the ramshackle street of weedy, debris-littered vacant lots broken up by the occasional house, and its murky windows of lamps on timers.

Jackoff and Asshole. *Jackson* Street and *Ashville* Street. We were fifteen, all of us, freshmen at Eight Mile High, though none of us were fresh in any meaning of that word. Out on a Friday night. Just *out*. My parents and Rita's down at the PCC getting hammered on cheap beer, as usual. The Polish Century Club—a windowless, cinder-block square they saw as the last outpost of the civilized in our ravaged neighborhood on the edge of Detroit. Ravaged. Savaged. Blighted. Slighted. Home.

Gene's father, recently dead from a gun to the head—looked like suicide, though the police weren't saying just yet. His mother didn't answer the phone, though we all knew she was holed up in that tiny box house. Gene's mother still had his younger stepbrother—this scrawny kid we called Sliver—at home. You wouldn't think she'd have motives—who'd want to get stuck with a dead guy's kid?—but I guess some thought she did. I bet they were talking about it that very moment down at the PCC. Gene spent the last week at my house in a sleeping bag on our basement couch while waiting for his own house to be vacated by the surly detectives who, according to Gene, wanted to call it a suicide and be done with it, but troubling facts kept getting in the way.

Rita and I had grown up together when every house was occupied and every check was embossed with the oval logo of Ford, the Chrysler penta-star, or the dull square block of GM. We all sang the Kumbaya of the Big Three. Rita's parents said I should call them Aunt and Uncle, but that never caught on with me. They seemed needy for affection, and that freaked me out. My father Leroy only shook hands, and then only on special occasions that required it. I had my own aunts and uncles. Rita, her parents' only child together, stood out as an oddity on our block of large Catholic families. A story there, but no one told us kids. I was one of three at home, plus my grandmother, so the street gave me breathing room and a different kind of wreckage.

On the chubby side, I was big enough to get teased for my tits in gym class. Rita, a bit plump back then, developed early, and thus caught the eye of a lot of the guys who had not experienced firsthand such development. So, our tits caught the eyes of the guys, but that's where similarities ended. She got a reputation for letting boys feel her up, and I got a reputation for ducking fights.

We still walked to school together, though the new architecture of our sprouting bodies threw awkward shadows over every word and gesture. Maybe we thought we were protecting each other, though if anything was keeping me safe, it was my ex-con Uncle Ted's reputation, hovering like a Rorschach cloud above me while the hoods studied it, trying to figure out how menacing it actually was.

Rita was lonely in that gray house with her drunken parents. At least my house had chaos going for it.

―――――――――

Jackson and Ashville. I stared into dark nothing and listened to low groans rumble beneath the light's pale buzz.

―――――――――

Jackson and Ashville. Gene leaned into Rita. Rita arched her back. October, a slight night chill. I glanced over and saw his hands snake up under her black T-shirt, their clumsy fluttering, unhooking, squeezing—whatever was going on under there was strangling me. The unzipping of her jeans stung my eyeballs, and then her sigh, and his jeans, and his groan. He said something, and she laughed. Reluctant sponge, I absorbed it. I could not wring myself out or flee or interrupt or sing doo-wop on that crumbling corner rounding into rubble.

You might wonder at how exposed they were—we all were—there where curb descended into sewer grate. Slow disintegration, the current method of urban renewal. Standards had deteriorated like our curbs so that only gunshots got anyone's attention. The handgun had made its appearance in our neighborhood to rave reviews.

Not so much an appearance as an invasion—like some Henry Ford of handguns was making sure they were affordable to every household in every hood, and every hood in every household. In order to have a conversation with a neighbor, you had to shoot off a gun first to get their attention. Then, they'd shoot off their gun, and then maybe you didn't need to have a conversation at all. Perhaps I exaggerate. In fact, I surely do exaggerate, for that is one of the useful skills of the slow and pudgy, the ability to stretch the truth enough to keep from getting your ass kicked. My point is, teenage groping on a street corner wouldn't cause any traffic jams. In fact, nothing could cause a traffic jam. The mass exodus to the further burbias by The Lucky Ones had already taken place years ago.

My point is, my point is. My point is that there was no point. No point at which Gene would come over to me and tap me on the shoulder and say, "Your turn," as planned.

I'd heard a rumor that the Smolinksi brothers had "tag-teamed" Rita at the Kiddie Park, the desolate, dilapidated playground next to St. Mike's, but couldn't muster the courage to bring it up with Rita. The Smolinskis. Denny—held back a year, repeated fourth grade, putting him in with his brother Buzz, concentrating the meanness into our grade. The school put them in separate classes, but that divide-and-conquer strategy failed miserably, spreading the Smolinski infection further through the building. St. Mike's was closed now due to lack of enrollment and now housed a methadone clinic and soup kitchen. The last nun leaving the convent had forgotten to turn out the lights. The church had taken their silver chalices and headed for the hills. Except we have no hills in Detroit, so they were either raised up in The Rapture or flew south like the geese were supposed to but no longer did.

I'm sorry to be making our streets so bleak. No more *desolate* or *dilapidated*. We had a sense of humor about it—Jackoff and Asshole—that I imagine was similar to that of kids in Communist countries. We didn't get the big picture, but the little picture didn't look so good, and was getting worse, so why not make fun of it, as if we had some control? Hee Hee. Ha Ha. Go fuck yourself and your mother too.

Jackoff and Asshole. I blew on my numb, red hands in that time-honored worthless gesture of the gloveless. I knew skin against skin could warm them up. I yanked my jean jacket tighter around me, which made me more aware of the loose flesh of my soft belly. At Metro Beach the previous summer, even my father had teased me about my boobs. My mother shushed him. My father had the hard body of a factory worker, though he was currently working in the kitchen of a Hoss's Steak House, having been laid off two years ago. Occasionally, he rustled up some steaks out the back door, and we asked no questions as we wolfed them down, the bloodier the better. Hoss himself had been dead twenty years—Hoss, a big guy who probably ate too many steaks for his own good. My father was hoping to get a job with the city picking up garbage—he had a connection on the inside. Their slogan was "Our Business is Always Picking Up!" and a truer slogan did not exist.

Gene had planned out the night, arranging to meet Rita under the streetlight at nine. We arrived first, watching Rita wade down against a thick wind scattering ticking leaves over concrete. My heart jumped or galloomped, or something—flickered like the damn streetlight—a thick rolling in my chest when I spotted her. I saw her every day, but never like this.

I loved Rita, okay. From kindergarten on, she'd always told me the truth. And I had kissed her under the torn awning of Bur-Ler's, our local department store, during a summer rainstorm the year we were going into seventh grade. We had stolen bubble gum together, though perhaps we should have lifted an umbrella instead. We chewed our gum and watched sheets of rain splash into potholes in the parking lot and billow under and through the awning. Our bare forearms touched as we leaned together away from the storm. I moved to kiss her. She took out her pink gum, and I took out mine. We threw our wads out into the rain and laughed and kissed.

Gene was a tall, thin spike in the air whose biggest claim to fame, up until his father's death, was *not* playing basketball, despite the entreaties of the principal and the coach at Eight Mile, who both seemed desperate for a winning record in something.

Being the first in our class to grow a moustache, Gene did not want to shave it off in order to play. It had already allowed him to purchase beer at a couple of places, though all the stores we could walk to were onto him now. He saw his future at age sixteen, when he could drive, as the buyer of alcohol for all cute girls. Those of us who could see beyond age eighteen simply dropped out of school. With no factory jobs left for our fathers, there was little hope for us. Someone had strangled the hands on time clocks everywhere, or stolen them and sold them for scrap.

———————

Jackson and Ashville. Are you still with me, blowing on your hands? When my grandfather died, he left me two $100 savings bonds. Should I take my inheritance and invest in a handgun, a little equalizer against the street?

Gene did tap me on the shoulder—to say "Let's go." He lit one of his father's cigarettes—*his* inheritance. Half a carton, and Gene planned on smoking them all himself. He had a theory behind that, but he wasn't sharing.

"What," I moaned under my breath, "about me?"

"She don't want you."

"What?" I asked again.

Jackson and Ashville. Jackoff and Asshole. No one was killed, but I'm stuck there now and forever.

———————

I ran to catch up with Rita, who had turned back up the street toward her house, the wind behind her now.

"Rita," I said, falling into step with her like I did each morning. But it was not morning, so where were we headed?

"EJ," she said. Three people on earth still called me EJ, and she was one of them.

"I thought, maybe . . ."

"EJ, no."

"What about the Smolinskis?"

She stopped walking and stared at me.

"I heard—" I halted, suddenly aware of the distant hiss of traffic from Eight Mile Road, where the cars always seemed to know where they're going.

"Earl," she said finally. "They tried to rape me."

I let out a long stream of hot breath. A lot of things slipped by in our neighborhood, but not rape.

"Did . . . Did you call the cops?"

We were suddenly in front of her house, and I wasn't nearly done catching up.

She stared harder. She touched my face, and everything inside me tightened.

"Earl, I said yes to Gene so I could say no to you." Each time she used my real name, I flinched. She turned and walked up the stoop to her dark house and slipped her key in the lock and disappeared. A light came on strong and bright through the thick curtains, against all odds.

Drunk Driving Down Memory Lane

Bad shit happens in cars. It was once easy to find alternate routes, unmarked deviations to keep memories from idling too high, but then, what? Traffic, fender-benders, the mad acceleration into a permanent stall, the heart towed away for scrap.

My brother Vince drove me to the airport. State police directed us away from an explosion of sirens ahead of us. *Think somebody just died*, I said, crossing myself. Checked the papers the next day to confirm. I can go on with car metaphors all day, having grown up in the Motor City. Let's start with hoods and trunks, right? Vince going 5 over the limit, as is the custom in much of the free world, but we ground to a shocked crawl, rubbernecking, gawking, silent with accumulated exhaust.

On Eight Mile, I slammed to a stop in the left turn lane, motor running, got out, and stomped away down the weedy median. My girlfriend Angie and her sister Ginger still in the car. Angie and I had fought over a piece of good news— hearing the *asshole* in my own voice, embarrassed with Ginger listening, the world leaning into their horns.

Stalking memory, I drive out of my way to find places I parked with lovers, looking for lack of streetlights, odd dead ends, high hedges, twisted street signs and twisted sweet sighs, but they've been trimmed back, erased on the past's GPS, or maybe never happened.

My Plymouth Satellite broke down on the I-96 entrance ramp, and Willie Warren, committed to helping with gas money back to Detroit, instead got out of the car, walked off, started hitching. Fuck you, Willie—no sign of the cross for you.

On I-75, I dropped my drive shaft near the bulletproof Kentucky Fried off Livernois, a delayed reaction to drunk-driving through a park fence— thought I'd gotten away with it. The tow-truck guy wanted a tip for picking it up in that blighted neighborhood. When he dumped me at my apartment, I gave him the beers from my fridge and a bad check I later made good on.

We try to make good on the bad shit, and suddenly we're out of change at the last pay phone in America, the tank on E, the heater on Hopeless. Try making the sign of the cross. It might make you feel better—even a half-assed cross, depending on who else is in the car, who else is ready to abandon you.

Teeter-Totter

I had always liked him. I made my first communion right behind him in second grade, all of us lined up, in angelic order. One of my earliest memories is staring at his slicked-back hair as we waited in the vestibule and smelling the hair tonic his mother had slathered on him like holy oil.

Brad Pollak. Last I heard he was an alcoholic living on the streets of Ann Arbor. You might say that I sure knew how to pick him, but everyone picked him back then. The boys picked him first when they were picking up teams, if he wasn't doing the picking himself. He was probably the one they picked to do the picking, I can't say for sure, watching from the merry-go-round on the Kiddie Park at St. Mike's Elementary down on Eight Mile. The girls oohed and aahed over him well before we knew what to do next, after the oohing and aahing.

On the playground, he occasionally made fun of my name, Mirabelle, though otherwise paid me no mind. He was a pioneer in our school, introducing the French Kiss at a 6th grade spin-the-bottle party. It caused a certain amount of hysteria among the girls, as I heard in the girls' bathroom—I heard, because I—a shy, late-bloomer immigrant from, gasp, Canada—was not invited to the party. That insertion of the tongue—most agreed it was pretty great. "You're French," Penny, one of the Kiski twins, said, "I bet you know how to do it." They all laughed. She swirled her tongue around to demonstrate and caused such squealing that Sister Patrice swished her black habit into the bathroom and whirled us all back into the hallway like the wicked witch that she was.

In grade school, he once claimed my name meant Daisy Duck in French. Another day, Brad said he'd looked it up and it meant "Wonderful Tax Collector." In our neighborhood of mostly Polish Catholics, no one knew what to make of my name, though I knew not a lick of French. My name almost defined me back then—irrelevant and suspicious.

I was named after my grandmother, and though I attempted to Americanize it in school to "Mary," the nuns were having none of it— no messing around when it came to the Virgin's name. My mother told me it meant "wonderful" in French, though that's a lie. It means a kind of plum, or Tinker Bell. When Brad and I moved across the road from St. Mike's to Eight Mile High for ninth grade, we were the only Catholic school kids tracked into level-3 math, the lowest. I told him the secret of my name when we were paired together working on story problems. It was his idea of flirting to tell everyone in that class of strangers that my name meant Tinker Bell and watch me blush. I should have been paying more attention to his ideas.

Maybe I was thrilled that he had noticed me—between eighth and ninth grade, I had blossomed. That's the word the adults used. My father's factory friends either stared openly at my breasts or turned away, depending on where their wives were or how many beers they'd drunk.

"You were one of the good girls with invisible haloes," Brad said, recalling our time at St. Mike's as if it had ended a lifetime ago, not just a matter of months. I remember when being married to God suddenly started to seem like a pretty rotten deal. Most of us in that communion line at some point probably expressed a desire to be a nun or priest, but by sixth grade, we'd moved on to bigger sins—except for Ellen Loretish, who did indeed become a nun, and Mary Neal, who married one. Catholic school is a pile of clichés, most of them true. By the time we ripped up and dumped all of our school papers and workbooks in the coat closet in back of our classroom at the end of 8th grade, we were ready for new ways of spinning the bottle.

———————

Brad started drinking early too, adding to his infamous repertoire. I think maybe he flamed out into ash because he started everything too early, foot on the gas, no interest in braking.

I know it sounds stupid. Has always sounded stupid, but I did sort of want to be a bad girl. Brad was like a slow leak of blue ink spreading over the neatly lined sheets of loose leaf in our binders. I wasted a lot of ink on that boy trying to tell this story.

Rita stabbed him in the back with the point of her compass in fourth grade, and for years I wished she'd had the grace to push it all the way in and save us all a lot of trouble. I got rid of that invisible halo a long time ago. I admit, last time I drove through Ann Arbor on my way to the hospital for more tests, I looked for him on the streets, not to help him, but to buy him a drink, if you know what I mean. But hey, I'm in the Cancer Club now, so I want to get it right this time and not waste any more paper.

———————

Lurking by my locker one afternoon that fall, Brad asked if I wanted to hang out with him on Saturday. Our last names seemed to be keeping us in proximity forever. We were in homeroom together too.

"What does hanging out with Brad Pollak mean?" I asked, packing up my books and waiting for the Kiski twins to walk home with me, as usual. I could see them just then, turning the corner down C corridor where our ninth grade lockers were. October, freshman year, and falling leaves had become an afterthought to us. Everything was new, new, new—school dances where we could slow dance tight with boys free from the nuns' dark shadows.

"I don't know," he said, surprising me. He suddenly wasn't the one shining star—or one shining stud—that he was over at St. Michael's. At Eight Mile High, our freshman class of three hundred was nearly the size of grades one through eight at St. Mike's. He was trying to figure out his game plan, I think, for the larger field. And who was I, a referee? A reliable benchwarmer he was finally calling into the game? His confidence had been shaken and stirred by a junior jock who had pinned him up against his locker and threatened him, just because. Just because was reason enough at Eight Mile, and we all learned that pretty quick.

"We can go over to the park, you know. Just hang out."

No boy had ever given me such a vague invitation. I didn't know what my parents would say.

"Meet me on the corner of Jackson and Ashville," I said. "Okay?"

"Great," he said. I noticed thick veins roped through his thin, muscled arms. It was jacket weather, but he still wore short sleeves.

I knew the Kiski twins from first grade, and though we no longer wore uniforms, I think we saw the invisible St. M's crest on each other's foreheads—familiar, haloed or unhaloed, scattered among the thick hordes that crushed down the halls when the bells rang. Eight Mile had near-daily fights in that mad commotion—fights no nuns could have broken up. Girl fights too, and we at St. Mike's rarely fought. Maybe we should have, instead of repressing every single physical urge. We didn't have a gym. No phys ed to sweat out our sins.

"What does hanging out with Brad Pollak mean?" I asked them as we walked past Bur-Ler's, then Glabicki's funeral home, our familiar apostrophes of ownership. They looked at each other, then at me.

From here on in, all I have are these flashes. Time breaks down. The clock takes some drugs on a dare. The hands turn to rubber. The numbers blur into graffitied obscenities.

I walked slowly down our sidewalk to join him at the corner. I'd been peeking out the window like an idiot. Brad immediately put his arm around me, and I quickly turned to look back to see if my mother was watching. I wish now that she had been.

"Stop," I said. He just smiled and turned to me, raising his open hands at what I was slow to realize was breast level. "Stop," I said again, grabbing his hands, yanking them down.

Why didn't I turn then, go right back up the sidewalk and into my house? Brad Pollak, and it was a beautiful fall day, and I was a wonderful tax collector.

It saddens me to know that he must not remember any of this, he who was both one of my first memories and one of my worst.

"C'mon, Daisy Duck," he said. "I can't help myself."

We kissed, my back against a tree. Mound Park was smaller than some of the front lawns of mansions on Jefferson Avenue in Grosse Pointe where people named Ford and Chrysler lived. In my mind, that park has shrunk further to the size of an oriental rug or perhaps an above-ground swimming pool, but it must have been bigger. A playground with swings, two slides, a merry-go-round, and two teeter-totters. I haven't driven past since my mother died fifteen years ago. In fact, I've devised detours around it. My therapist—yes, I see one—and my husband—yes, I'm married—both think I should go back and slay the demons.

What do they know? There's just one demon, and it quietly fed off the sparse greenery of that sad park, growing enormous until I finally had to give it a name.

We sat on either end of a teeter-totter. "How many times have you played on one of these? Once or twice? Once, if the guy on the other end got off and let you slam to the ground like a chump."

"That never happened to me," I said. "But I saw it happen in the Kiddie Park." The Kiddie Park at St. Michael's—where the Recess Mothers patrolled the muddy landmines at the bottom of the slides, the beaten path around the merry-go-round, the monkey bars where I chipped a permanent tooth.

We were politely bouncing up and down. "It takes cooperation," I said. "You have to be equal to make it work."

"If it's equal, you don't move at all. You both just stand with your feet on the ground. What fun is that?"

"I like it like this," I said. "Gentle." He was too far away to touch me. I felt safe. I knew he wasn't going to jump off. Why would he do that?

A pure buzz surged through my body with the understanding that I had power over him—his mad lust. I had never felt that power before—or hadn't let myself feel it. And if we could've eased off then, and walked back through the narrow park and back to the clean new sidewalk they'd laid the length of Ashville Street with tax money from the Chrysler plant, it might've been one of the happier days of my life.

I had been tugged by Brad Pollak nearly all my life—heart-tugged to get a look, a laugh, the time of day, a second of a minute of the time of day, the click of a camera shutter from him.

Oh, I was a wonderful tax collector. It was lonely work. No one to pat me on the back and say, Well done.

When Brad turned the corner onto Jackson, the long, flat straight mile connecting Ryan Road to Mound, I could stand and watch him all the way to Ryan, and I did, until he became a speck disappearing behind the Baptist Church Kar Wash on the corner.

When Jackson hit Mound, it dead-ended at the Chrysler plant. The last address on Ashville was for the Eight Miles High Bar, where I often spotted my father's car in the rutted dirt parking lot.

"I shot pool with your dad in Eight Miles High," Brad said. The drinking age then was eighteen, but still, that was ridiculous.

I wanted to tell him he was lying. How could he get in a bar at age fifteen? Why would my father play pool with someone he must have recognized from St. Mike's—my father, an old ex-jock who had been the assistant coach of the CYO team.

"Wasn't he your football coach?" I asked. "I mean . . ."

"That's why he played pool with me, his old star running back!" Brad said. "Why else?" Brad asked. "He even vouched for me with the bartender," he added, and suddenly I knew it was true. I could see my father doing it.

"He's mad at me for not joining the Eight Mile team," he added. And I knew that was true too. Brad wasn't a supernatural athlete, but he was our star. Pride of the SaMy Lions. Yeah, SaMy, for St. Mike's—you think I could make up something like that?

The float party was in Gene Wrobleski's garage—that was our excuse for hanging out, to help build the 9th grade float. I can't remember the homecoming theme or what our float actually ended up resembling once all the flowers were tied on to the chicken wire. Probably something about cartoons—Eight Mile High was in denial about what was going on: three girls that I know of got pregnant that year. A teacher was one of the fathers. In addition to the drinking age being lowered from 21 to 18, our hallways were filled with drug dealing, and drug wars among the dealers. They finally started bringing in the drug-sniffing dogs, but then it all just moved out to the parking lot.

"Float party" came to be a euphemism—the first thing I remember seeing in air quotes—for any kind of bad behavior. I realized rather quickly that all-night cosmic bowling was a similar code for my children's generation.

Homecoming was one week away, so the class officers had float parties scheduled all weekend to try and catch up. I'd been to a couple of the nighttime gatherings where people stood around and flirted with each other and nothing got done. Our class president Gene—elected by the eighth graders in the junior high without any Catholic input—was the only freshman capable of growing a moustache, and that seemed to have earned him the admiration of both the boys and the girls. Brad had some work to do to get elected—he'd immigrated to the new country of Eight Mile High where his cool passport was no longer recognized.

We walked up the driveway toward the wood and chicken-wire skeleton with a few paper flowers tied on. The day's activity was to make hundreds more tissue flowers.

"Let's get out of here," Brad said almost immediately. I saw the Kiski twins folding pink tissues into roses and tying them on to a shapeless blob that could have been anything at that point. One of the twins waved to me. I don't know which one, and suddenly it didn't really matter. On the edge of being rescued, I let myself be willingly led into deeper water.

———————

Brad stopped and turned to face me as soon as we were behind the park's rusted cyclone fence and past the first row of trees. Old trees from before the subdivision was built. When this was all part of someone's farm. They'd saved a few for this small park—large, established, beautiful in fall. We'd collected leaves here on a field trip from St. Mike's, the nuns almost giddy to be outside without restriction.

———————

The invisible halo has always been a problem for me. And in angry flashes, I sometimes blame it on the nuns. I had to wear a Kleenex on my head in church once when I'd forgotten my hat. I remember that as vividly as first communion—the disappointment of the dry wafer. We'd never talked about the taste. Shouldn't it be good? Shouldn't we want more of it?

———————

He pulled me to him and brought his lips to mine. I laughed, giddy with shock.

"What are you doing?"

"Kissing you," he said. "Don't you want to?"

Such a simple question, but it had me stumped.

"Yes," I said. "I think. But not like this." I felt blood rising in my face with excitement and confusion. "Let's walk," I said. Even in movies where time and romance speeded up, it never seemed so sudden and without emotion. The physical act completely separate from feeling. Spin the bottle was one thing—well, I didn't really know, did I?—but this seemed like quite another.

———————

"Like how," he said. "How do you want me to kiss you?" He grabbed me again and pulled me against him so I could feel his hardness. I pulled back.

When you've known someone since kindergarten—rape didn't enter my mind, but Brad was scary out-of-control, like he'd taken me into this little city jungle of trees, and he was the king of that jungle. What happened to the power I'd felt earlier? I had a lot to learn back then—I want to take that girl and shake her. I want to show her how to wedge keys between her fingers into a claw.

He tilted his head back and sighed like I was disappointing him. Like I didn't understand the point he was making. Like I was too dumb.

It must have been hours that we tangled and untangled like unruly prickly bushes back and forth through Mound Park. He had pulled my blouse out of my jeans and tried to reach his hands inside my bra. My wrists were circled with red blotches from his hands pulling mine down. I ended up with bruises, as if I had tried to kill myself with dull naivety. Or stupidity.

I could see the simple, uncomplicated street from between the trees, yet I felt stuck in an overgrown maze. Desire and fear. Why couldn't I sort it out?

It's the kind of story women tell in groups, when they've maybe had too much to drink. Maybe they're lonely. Maybe ashamed of something in their life now. They go back to moments with a boy in a car, in a house with the parents gone, in the woods, behind a garage. Moments they wished to have back.

I've taken my clothes off and had sex with a number of men, but never in a city park in the middle of the day. I've never seen someone so mad with lust as that boy. Sometimes I think if I'd just played it right, I could have used that power I'd so quickly given up—could've had him licking my feet, rolling over like a submissive dog in the grass, showing me his belly, letting me decide whether to scratch it or not.

———————

When I showed the Kiski twins the bruises from where he held me, I wanted someone to understand that I'd fought him off. "You should have warned me," I hissed.

"You shouldn't tell anyone," Penny or Jenny said. "It'll get twisted. Boys always twist everything around."

———————

He yanked open two buttons on my purple blouse, so roughly that one came loose, hung by a thread, then fell into the dust. I wish I could remember him saying one thing that exuded some kind of charm, something beyond what I learned soon afterwards were stale clichés.

———————

Two young boys with dirty faces and ragged T-shirts raced through the park, laughing outrageously, high-pitched and mad. One may have been chasing the other, or they were co-conspirators fleeing some minor vandalism or cruelty, I couldn't tell. Brad turned and watched, laughing softly, for a moment almost distracted.

"I don't remember you being like that," I said.

"Oh, yeah, sure," he said, smiling, "we were always running wild."

"You're being like that now," I said, harsh and sudden. "Today. With me."

"This, this is different," he said, with exaggerated gestures, taken aback, almost as if I'd hurt his feelings. "We didn't care about girls back then." As if that explained anything.

"You're rough like those boys," I said, jabbing my fingers through the air in their direction. Boys were afraid of each other, the pecking order based on size and brute strength. And they picked on the smaller ones, the shyer ones, the ones with lisps, the ones with glasses. Until they turned their attention to girls.

"You're like those boys," I repeated. "Except not innocent."

"I deserve better." With a fierce surge of some primal force, I pulled my arm back and went to punch him, but he grabbed my fist and forced it down.

"This isn't about what you deserve. It's about what you want," he said. "Why," he asked, continuing to shackle my wrist, "Why did you meet me?"

"Not to get raped," I shouted. Despite myself, tears flew from my cheeks.

"Whoa, whoa," he said. "I didn't rape you. We haven't done anything."

"Then back off," I said. I pulled away and looked at my nicest blouse that I'd worn special to meet him. I'd never wear it again. "I thought I liked you," I said. I wanted to say more, but I had to choke back sobs. "Look at me," I said, but he wouldn't.

The only path through the park was littered with wood chips to keep the mud down. The dirty chips spread thin over the worn path—more the idea of a safe path than anything. Brad picked up a handful and threw them hard against a tree, but when you throw something light, it's hard to get much force, so they fluttered down quickly, disappearing in high weeds.

Those boys either did not see us, or did not care.

Through the thickening mirage of dusk, I walked back up the driveway to the float party alone. The paper flowers glowed, spilling out of large, clear plastic bags, under the garage floodlight. It reminded me of first communion. The excess whiteness, the illusion of purity. The bright, hard hosts. I can feel one on the roof of my mouth, even today, stuck. I wait for its slow disintegration.

I pressed my hands together. I bowed my head and entered the light. A couple of drunk 9th grade boys were throwing handfuls of paper flowers in the air as I made my way toward the garage. President Gene, even with his moustache and deep voice, seemed powerless to stop them, or perhaps he didn't care.

"We're not hurting anybody," one of them shouted.

Baptism by Fire

My parents smoked: Marlboros, Kools. Matchbooks stacked or spilled in the cupboard, slipped into my pocket heading out into the abstract theory of night. I lit one match, set the whole pack on fire. One big hiss on our snakeless streets. One big flame that burned out quick. Sixteen, trying out for love, getting cut for not knowing the playbook. Both cut, we invented a game based on guilt and doubt. In other words, a new religion to replace what we'd abandoned. Fire: the only thing I liked about the old one. Altar boy. Candles lit/ candles extinguished. A little power on God's stage. In the yard on Jackson Street, burn barrel half-filled with ash wet from rain. Sixteen, I had my permit, not my license. Ragged edge of newspaper singed. Cardboard box of frozen peas. Business-sized envelopes I had no business with. Mongrel mutt at my feet. Nothing redundant. Lame vocabulary of lined matches. In my hand, a transistor-radio box filled with girls' notes and school pictures. Sixteen, not such a big box, but I'd saved them, evidence of past romance, present sin, for she wanted no past, her Eve to my

Adam—abused twice, I later learned, erasing her own history, so why should I have mine? Even the dog sniffed, knowing to burn them was wrong. That's a stretch, but in our manufactured melodrama, the rattling tin cans of tears tore through the syrupy silence of what we imagined was love. We kept cutting each other from the team. Who needed a coach? Why save them? Can I read them? I'd had sex with two of them. Okay? Enough? Too much. The dog, her stand-in, and even he knew. The earliest ones folded tightest, like paper footballs passed in classes. Punted. *My sister likes you. Meet me after school behind Dairy Queen. Bring your kisses. My parents will be out late. Do you like me? Do I like you?* Paper footballs into flames. School pictures I longed to keep, and their small tight paragraphs of inked praise. Cheap shame, and my first wallet was empty, no way to buy my way out. Behind the garage, hands not warming over lame flames in the garbage can poked with holes for air to feed the fire. The radio, AM-FM, telescoping antenna to pick up hard-rock FM, AM ballgames, and bad news. Sixteen, an idiot arsonist for love. We needed a coach, but we'd been cut. How to destroy all evidence of destroying all evidence? My heart misbehaved, swollen into the bad apple, shriveled to the bad seed. The bored dog peed against the fence and trotted away. The gates to the garden—were we locked in or out? It took another pack of matches to finish the job. The job never finished. I didn't want any bitter shred of sweet old news. Who'd told us we could only have one love? Some stupid song on AM? Thank God it didn't end well. Sixteen—such a burden to lighten your load. I needed ballast of early kisses. New ash rose stiff off the damp pile. My fingers blackened with the deed. Don't get me started on how long I spent scrubbing them.

Timber

Earl was crouched in the second seat of the family station wagon, his face crushed against the window. Rain sprayed off the glass and roof like an endless drum solo in the middle of a dull concert, the rest of the band fleeing to the dressing room to get stoned, forgetting to come back. Was the drummer going to give up, throw his drumsticks to the crowd and walk off stage? No, he was not. He kept pounding, rain streaming down for the three hours they'd been on the road—one more before they arrived at Timber Shores Campground for a week's vacation.

"Can't we listen to the radio?" Earl asked in his sullen teenage voice, undercut slightly by a hint of squeaky whine. The Styrofoam cooler and grocery bags of food on the seat crowded Earl against the door.

"Shut up back there," his father said. "I can't see shit." He turned the wipers down, then up again.

"Your father's driving," his mother wheeled around. "Let him concentrate." Then, softer, to Earl's father. "Leroy, already with the swearing?" She was puffing her cigarette like a jerky stoner who just got kicked out of a high school dance. In fact, like Earl himself. "Honey, we're on vacation, remember?"

"You want to drive, Ann?" his father asked.

Earl wanted to ask his mother for a smoke. Instead, he stuffed his mouth with stale orange circus peanuts, a strange marshmallow concoction they always had piled in plastic bags near the entrance to Valu Time. Something cheap and sweet his mother picked up to bribe his younger siblings, Vince and Alice, to behave. They swung on the cart, tossing sugary cereals in, hitting each other, screaming. Yep, Earl thought, his mother might want to drive.

Fifteen, Earl had been smoking for a couple of years, buying them at Max's Quik Last Stoppe Party Shoppe around the corner on Eight Mile. Max, the Polish madman, sold anything to anyone. Earl didn't even need to forge a note from his mother, though at first, Max only sold him Kools, his mother's brand. Earl had been such a regular, stopping in daily after his paper route, that Max ended up hiring him as a stock boy.

Vince, ten, and Alice, seven, were napping on a sleeping bag on the lowered third seat. Earl half-wished he could curl up back there and nod off with them, but those days were gone. He'd be embarrassed for his parents to see him sleeping.

Timber Shores had a sandy beach on Lake Michigan, a clubhouse, an unnecessary swimming pool, a teen center with dances, a minigolf course, a snack bar. All the amenities. And it had Peggy Fox. Earl and Peggy had become a couple—in the sudden way only young teenagers can—during the week their families had overlapped the previous summer: fast, full of shy, gooey affection and affectation, intermediaries and spies, faux-secret rendezvous, and even the traditional missives of love, which they had continued writing during the year apart. They'd become a couple based on campfires and pine scent, on ice cream and faux dry-humping.

Earl's father was proud of their step-up from state parks, where they'd camped for years in a musty canvas house tent. He was living large with his new "previously-owned" Apache pop-up camper at Timber Shores *Resort* Campground. The auto industry was booming, and Leroy was raking in the OT at Chrysler's. With his seniority, he managed to snag the primo second week in July for vacation—one of two weeks the "Fox Den" would be there—the Foxes from Cleveland came up every year with a caravan of friends and relatives. Earl's younger siblings had helped convince their parents to return to Timber Shores, the first and only time they vacationed in the same campground twice. Leroy saw it as a gesture to his teenage son. He had few gestures left at his disposal.

Rain, rain, go away. Rain, rain, please stay—Earl wasn't sure, his insides churning with circus peanuts and Peggy Fox.

Earl and his father set up the Apache in the rain while the others waited in the car. No hurrying his father—everything neat, level, zippers zipped, cranks cranked. The rain had slowed to a steady drizzle, and gray afternoon skies this far north were fading to the sincere black of night.

"Okay, we're good," his father finally said, clapping him hard on the back. Earl flinched, steadying his slight frame while his father brushed past him and gestured to the car for Ann and the other kids to come out. "Let's get some dinner going!"

Earl was hungry, but not hungry enough to stick around. He grabbed the last squished road sandwich from the cooler, then rushed out of their circle of campsites in Cluster 39 and up the dirt road in search of the Fox Den with their bulky luxury travel trailers. Out of breath, almost choking on the campground's fresh pine air, or on his last bite of slimy bologna, he saw Big Becca, in a screaming-yellow rain poncho, running up to him, before he even reached Cluster 45, as if she'd been assigned the role of scout in order to avoid a surprise attack from the savage boy from Detroit, a member of the Naïve tribe.

"Peggy already has a boyfriend this year," she said. Not *hi* or *great to see you again*. Earl began free-falling into a panic that verged on hyperventilation. Becca had practically *arranged* their coupling the previous year. "Becca Vicariously," he'd called her once. Peggy screwed up her face, so he hadn't said it again. Sixteen, Becca was a voyeuristic, matchmaking chaperone that Earl had no patience or pity for. Her name had never come up in the year of exchanging letters, yet here she was now defending the fortress against a friend who had come in peace.

Earl arched his feet and looked over her head through the trees into Cluster 45, scoping out the teenagers in a smaller cluster near the fire pit through thick patches of smoke. With what must have been wet wood, someone was trying to coax flames into catching. A tanned, sandy-haired boy in a tank top had his arm around Peggy. Earl's feet sank back into soft soil, the weight of a year's worth of anticipation nearly bringing him to his knees. All of his imagined cool over the capital G Girlfriend from capital O Ohio he'd told his friends about at Eight Mile High was driving him down into what was not sand at all but thick muck. His breath stuttered, and he gulped air to keep from drowning.

"His name is Beau," Becca said.

"Beau-*shit*," Earl said, and almost smiled, surprised by his own wit.

"That's foul," she said. "She's better off with Beau. You seem different. I can tell already."

"Maybe I am," he said, raising his voice so that heads turned from the campfire circle of dampness. "Or maybe I'm the same, and you guys don't know me at all. I was faking you out last year, like I was spelling Earl with an i and a flower for the dot," he said.

"Like a girl? Are you, like, a homo or something?"

"Is that what you call them in Cleveland?"

"That's what we call them in Michigan too, you homo," she said. They stood looking at each other levelly. "You're not even going to try to get her back?"

"Ask Peggy if I kissed her like a *homo*," Earl said. "Ask her about the *tongue*," he shouted.

"She said you don't know how to kiss," Becca said, and in her smug tone, her lowered voice, Earl could hear the truth. His felt the sudden sunburn of shame rise in his face.

"Tell her I'm a born-again Christian," he said. "Tell her I learned how to water-ski just for her. Tell her," he paused. She was stalking away. "Tell her I grew a big dick, just for her."

Becca stopped. She stood so still Earl could hear the lake kicking up waves in the unseen distance. But then she resumed walking. No moon, and he could not howl. His stomach hurt from telling lies. "Ask her about the tongue!" he shouted again.

"You—you don't deserve her. I'm not going to give her any messages," she said. "You'll have to ask her yourself."

"Ask her what? Ask her what?" but Becca was gone behind the curve of trees that led into 45. He managed to pull himself out of the quicksand and break into a wild sprint only to find himself trapped. Each cluster was a dead end, and the week ahead suddenly and hopelessly tangled like cassette tape pulled from its plastic case, the singer's voice garbled into gibberish.

———

For his birthday, Peggy sent him a lottery ticket from Ohio, and he'd won a free ticket. He'd carried it around with the three clovers in a row in his wallet's secret compartment next to the one rubber he'd managed to cadge from Jerry, the other stock boy at Max's.

Earl had planned to give her the ticket that week and have her mail him another one when she got home—a continuation, a commitment. A lucky charm. After some struggle, he yanked it out of the compartment and tore it to shreds. He littered and cursed. He kept the rubber. He wasn't much of a gambler.

———

The previous summer, they'd gotten together at the Monday night teen dance. On Thursday, Peggy's red-faced, beer-drinking bear of a father—either Rolfe or Ralph, depending on who was talking—had taken them out on his roaring, blustering hog of a ski boat.

"Just understand one thing," Rolfe said, as the boat shot straight out from the dock, cutting over choppy waves into the sharp wind, a rhythmic drop that forced Earl to hold onto the deck rail. Behind them, Peggy was pulling life jackets out of the hatch. Earl squinted. He thought her father was going to warn him about messing with his daughter, like they did on TV shows, but Rolfe said, "I'm a Buckeye and you're a Wolverine, little man, and the twixt don't go with the tween, if you know what I mean, and I hope you do. Did you watch The Game last year? We kicked your little Wolverine hiney good, and we're going to do it again this year, and I'll have my little girl Peggy here send you a personal message from me when it happens."

Earl had not watched The Game on TV—capital T capital G—as the annual Michigan-Ohio State football game was called. The boat was named Buckeye Nation XX, which Earl assumed meant that there were nineteen other boats named Buckeye Nation back in Ohio, where they had to make due with polluted Lake Erie.

"Sounds good." Earl shrugged, relieved. Peggy hit him with a life jacket. He put it on inside out and upside down. Back home, he didn't know anyone who had water skis or even a rowboat. The Detroit River was lined with warehouses and factories, and the closest he ever got to a body of water was Free Swim at the Eight Mile High pool on hot summer afternoons.

"You are a fan, aren't you?" Rolfe asked. "Every fool from Michigan is a Wolverines fan."

"Sure," Earl lied. He vaguely remembered being hungover that Sunday morning in November and reading about the missed field goal in the paper. The headline was either "Wide Left" or "Wide Right."

"It was wide, right?" Earl said.

"You got that right." Rolfe smiled a toothy grin and punched Earl hard in his right shoulder.

Earl was about to be introduced to an advanced level of humiliation—a new kind that multiplied itself by factors such as a girl and her father witnessing his complete hopelessness on water skis. They were going to give him a lesson. It would be fun, everyone said—even Earl's parents, happy to give him permission, to see him shy and smiling like he did when he was a boy.

How many times did Rolfe gun the boat to try to pull him up onto the skis? It was a cluster-fuck of falls. Earl could tell you himself if he wasn't busy gulping water after yet another face-plant slap onto the hard, glossy Lake Michigan surface, landscaped on that windy day like the white frosting on a cake his mother might ice for his birthday.

Rolfe was determined to get Earl up on skis at least once, but finally Peggy threw in his towel, where it floated on the surface, then disappeared. Or the towel fell in by accident. Or there was no towel because Earl had forgot to bring one, and when they pulled him into the boat like a trash fish they just wanted to cut loose, he shivered like a weenie until they got to shore, then ran straight to the special Timber Shores Boy's Room with its smiling Boy Moon on the door and peed long and hard and nearly cried.

When he got back to the Apache, stumbling over a tree stump in the dark, his mother scrambled to put a plate of dinner in front of him.

"Sorry," Earl managed.

"Actually, we thought you'd be gone longer," his mother said, smirking.

Their lantern hissed its soft impartial warmth from the picnic table. How could he tell them the whole week was already a bust?

"Well," Earl said. He shielded personal stuff from his mother. His father didn't seem to care, but here they all were, camp set up for a week at Timber Shores, for Earl to pick up where he left off. He sat down and hung his head.

"She's already, you know, with somebody," he managed without tears.

"Oh, sweetie, not the girl who sent you all those cute letters?"

"You read them?" he flashed.

"No—well, just ones you left lying around."

"Tramp," his father said, exhausted from the drive.

"Twamp," Alice said. Back home, she took speech class for her R's. They tried not to laugh, but then laughed.

"From Ohio," his father said, as if that explained everything.

"That was fun," Peggy said around the Buckeye Nation campfire, Earl in dry clothes, but Peggy still in her neon-orange bikini. She had a killer body of curves, and Earl could blatantly stare at it in the dim flicker of firelight. "You were cute," she said. "You tried so hard." Peggy, who skied one handed, one-footed, backward, and was working on upside down.

The Buckeye Nation was into Budweiser and Coke and all things All-American. The large group of men and women cackled and guffawed with their beers in red Buckeye beer cozies while the teenagers sipped Cokes and the younger ones burned marshmallows.

"What do you do in Cleveland?" Earl asked.

"I go to school, you dork," Peggy said, and she and Becca laughed.

"So much for small talk," Becca said. "You should kiss her," she whispered. "Go for a walk and kiss her." They gratefully got up and wandered off onto the dark campground road, feet shuffling through dusty gravel, arms around each other's hips. Earl's hand rested on the soft flesh there. That small warm contact sent his frenzy into high alert. "Oh, man," he said aloud. Other campfires from other clusters glowed through trees. He leaned back against a sappy pine off to the side near the fake-log-cabin bathhouse and pulled her to him. They kissed. A gob of pinesap stuck to the back of his head, and he lost his place.

He reached back to try to pull it out of his hair. "It must be a metaphor," he said.

"A meteor?" she laughed. "You're so romantic." He thought to correct her, but she leaned in and gave him some tongue.

It was this moment he'd replayed for nearly a year on unforgiving concrete streets, in dull classrooms, and in his stuffy bedroom on the top bunk above a snoring Vince. He had planned how he was going to say, "Remember that meteor we saw last year?"

Earl fiddled with the telescoping antenna on his tiny AM-FM transistor. He'd taken his hidden joints out of the battery compartment and replaced them with the solid rectangular battery. Earl was a listener of WABX-FM, the "underground" station in Detroit, but he couldn't pick up the signal that far north, where Detroit was a whispered rumor of industrial smoke signals that dissipated into vague relief that it was indeed a long day's drive away. The only rock station he could pick up was CKLW-AM, "the Big Eight" on your dial, the top-40 station out of Windsor, Canada, across the bridge. CKLW had an enormous antenna, bigger than those allowed in the States. Their hourly news squawked about gruesome murders in Detroit. While the station had helped spread Motown music across the Midwest, it also helped Detroit get labeled Murder City.

Earl sat at a picnic table in the middle of Cluster 39 listening to the Big Eight's syrupy bubble-gum pop, far from their campsite at the outer edge. Their tiny pop-up camper had no hiding places. He'd wrapped his joints tightly in Valu Time plastic wrap. Earl noticed that brands missing letters or with extra letters were often inferior or in some way deficient. He'd rubber-banded tight around the plastic wrap, since it had absolutely no cling. He worried that the rolling papers would tear. He was going to check. Maybe light one up, take a couple hits.

Then, Peggy and Becca snuck up from behind and rushed at him with tickling hands. Becca's stubby claws dug into his ribs.

"Give, I give," he shouted, shoving the joints into the pocket of his cut-offs as he squirmed away, knocking the radio to the dirt. The Buckeye

Nation was not into pot. The one kid his own age in their group was an Eagle Scout. Well-scrubbed and earnest, they had all the flavor and false cheer of a TV sitcom.

"You guys scared me," Earl said.

Peggy picked up his radio. "Hey, CKLW," she said. "I didn't know you could get a Cleveland station all the way up here!"

"Cleveland?" Earl said.

"Yeah, Cleveland-KLW," Peggy said, "Duh."

"They're always talking about those murders in Detroit though," Becca said. "It's not safe like Cleveland." They were from Shaker Heights and rarely went into the city. "Nobody gets murdered in Cleveland."

"What's the KLW stand for?" Earl asked. "Clue?" He attributed Peggy's obliviousness to her love of catchy pop tunes. She was always humming or singing one, swaying those sweet hips that made him forget anything she might have said or was in the process of saying.

"Why are you in Cluster 39?" she asked. "What Michigan player wears 39?"

"Yeah," Becca said. "We stay in 45, Archie Griffin's number."

"Meeeshigan," Earl said, clueless. "Maize and blue. Crystal blue persuasion," he sang, "Hmmm, good vibrations."

"It's *a new vibration,*" they both immediately corrected.

"I got one for you," Earl said, taking Peggy's hand in his. He needed a touchstone, something to ground him in Buckeye Land. "What's a Shondell?"

They both stared. Peggy scrunched up her nose like she was trying to read a foreign language. "It's a good thing you're so cute!" she said.

"Ditto," he said.

The joints went unsmoked in Year One. They crumbled in Valu Time and he took them back to Warren, where he re-rolled them in new papers and smoked them at an Allman Brothers concert at Cobo Hall where the

Brothers got mad when the crowd booed off their warm-up act, John Hammond, so they refused to play "Whipping Post" as an encore.

He packed new joints, better joints for Year Two. A rubber, three joints, the lottery ticket—three forms of I.D., and he didn't know which he would or could use.

Becca. Why was he mean to her? Why did everyone treat her like the last one to be picked when no one was playing that kind of game anymore?

Or, maybe they were. A chubby girl like her would not get picked first in kickball or kissing games. Even Peggy treated her poorly, asking her to fetch a Coke, fix her hair, or, once, a simple, abrupt, "Shut up."

Earl felt bad about letting her take the brunt of his angry flash, trying to pass the humiliation on to her. He said nothing—not one word—to Peggy the entire week, avoiding her in that small country, that tiny island of bored teenagers trying to get away from their parents.

During the long year of writing letters, he'd convinced Peggy that CKLW was from Canada, not Cleveland. Their exchanges got shorter and shorter, and the distance from their kissing and half dry-humping lengthened and faded into an idea, not a physical thing. She'd stopped dotting her I's with hearts in the spring, which made him all the more desperate to see her again in summer. She'd sent him her school picture, air-brushed, perfect, breasts swelling tight against a pink sweater. In his fantasies, he and Peggy weren't doing much talking.

On the second night of the week in the second year, just like the previous year, the Teen Dance took place in the Teen Center. Anyone who wanted to find romance at Timber Shores needed to get started at the Monday dance. Earl hovered in the shadowy scent of nearby pines. Moping. He was mopey dopey. He'd smoked his first doobie. He was a dope for spending a year sending letters to Peggy Fox/1743 Richland Dr./Shaker Heights, OH 44109, telling her about squeaky clean Earl Rhodes, carefully omitting all references to drinking or smoking pot, or even WABX, in his workman-like accounts of his school year. He wondered if hers were as heavily edited as his. He'd had no girlfriends, but a fair number of boozy kisses at Eight Mile parties.

Maybe it was the idea of Peggy he liked—that he could have a nice wholesome girlfriend in Ohio who thought he was nice and wholesome himself, even if he couldn't water ski, even though he didn't give a shit about "The Game." A girl who didn't think "he'd be a nice guy if he wasn't so stoned all the time," as Ellen Loretish, one of his high school classmates, had told his mother in the Valu Time while she rung up the family shopping cart one rainy day in March and made his mother cry and his father ground him. Even though Peggy might have told him the same thing if she knew how much he partied, he could construct another version of himself for her, a version he could maintain, at least on paper.

Earl would've had long hair like his friends if his father let him grow it out, but the short, clippered cut was one reason he'd fit in with the Buckeye Nation. His father had always cut Earl's hair, and they'd nearly come to blows over it when Earl looked in the mirror after the most recent hatchet job.

———————

Maybe it was the idea of himself—that he could change his life, dial it back a couple of years, erase his shit-eating grin back to aw-shucks. He'd started drinking and smoking pot in junior high at St. Michael's. Back home, everyone knew he was a stoner, but at Timber Shores, for one week, he didn't have to be one. For one year of edited letters, he didn't have to be one. But what did he want to be? Not an Eagle Scout. The joints in the radio compartment were his batteries now, his antenna tuned in to a more narrow range of stations.

––––––––––––

From under the eaves of the teen center, a pale, wispy dark-haired girl with raccoon eyes stared at him. When Earl looked up and held her gaze, she wandered over to stand beside him. She had a slick Detroit slouch he recognized. He'd been waiting for Peggy and Beau. Was he going to make a scene? Pick a fight with freckle-faced Beau? Beau was one of those campground kids who went barefoot all the time and acted like he owned the place, even if he'd only been there a week. Beau—what kind of sissy name was that?

––––––––––––

"What are you doing here?" the girl asked. "You look like the thing that doesn't belong in a puzzle in *Highlights* in the dentist's office."

Earl was silent. *She* seemed like the thing that didn't belong—her peasant blouse, bellbottoms low on her narrow hips, frayed edges dragging on the ground, Frisbee tucked into the back of her pants, glowing in the dark.

"Hey cool cat, what cat's got your tongue?" she asked.

"I'm shipwrecked on an island full of mutineering Buckeyes," Earl said.

"Are you stoned?" she asked, sniffing close to his chest. "Because if you are, I would really like to get stoned also."

"It's buried treasure," he said. "But I forgot where I buried it."

"My name is Emmma," she said. "Three m's. Let's go find it."

"No name in the world has three m's," Earl said. They were already drifting away from the muffled thump of the teen dance. "You ever know anyone named Beau, like B-E-A-U?"

"Gum tastes better with sand in it," Vince said, chewing a big wad. "Crunchy."

They were playing tetherball at the beach. He'd covered his arms with blurry Bazooka Joe tattoos.

"You having fun, Earl?" Vince asked. "Mom and Dad are worried you're not having fun. Dad says we came back here just because of you and now you're being all snotty because of that ugly girl . . ." He stopped to blow a giant bubble. Earl reached over and popped it.

"She's not ugly. What the hell you talking about?" He smacked the ball at a severe angle so Vince couldn't reach it, and the rope whipped around the pole. Vince jumped futilely as the ball circled till it bounced tight against the pole, then slowly unwound.

"Snotty," Vince repeated. "And we have to share our campfires in the middle of the cluster. And she has a big fat butt."

"What?" Earl said. "Wait, what?" Vince was building up momentum just like that ball at an angle. Sometimes he wondered at the age gap between him and Vince. What was going on between his parents in those five years?

"What girl you talking about?"

"We have to share our campfire with everybody. Daddy can't even build it the way he wants. Got some crazy rednecks shooting charcoal lighter all over the place, then they get drunk and piss on the fire and we have to go in the Apache and cover our ears while you're out being snotty. You can be snotty at home, and it's a lot cheaper, Mom says. And I don't like roasting marshmallows in front of other people. I don't want other people critiquing my marshmallows."

"Critiquing?" Earl said. "Where'd you pick up a word like that?"

"No fun," Vince said. "And you've got Teen Central and everything."

"Teen Center," Earl said. Vince was right. His parents had thrown him a bone by returning to Timber Shores, and what was he doing with it? He was burying it in the toxic waste dump of self-pity. Had he thanked them for the bone? He had not. He let Vince win the next two games.

When Vince realized Earl was tanking, he stormed away, kicking sand, running toward Alice, who was working on a giant sand castle with a bunch of younger kids. The Eagle Scout was helping.

Earl gave the ball one more half-hearted smack and wandered off to look for Emma.

In the morning, Earl woke to the smell of bacon sizzling on the Coleman stove. The others were still asleep in the tight confines of the Apache, Vince and Alice sprawled on the foldout dinette set. Earl lay on one extended wing, and his father lay on the other, his back toward Earl, curled up in his sleeping bag. His mother had snuck out to get breakfast started. He had a feeling he might never, after this week, go camping with his family again. Part of him thought that'd be just fine, but the other part quietly rose and slipped into his jeans and stepped outside to sit beside his mother. She was smoking a cigarette with one hand and dripping greasy strips of bacon onto paper towels with the other. Years later, after his mother quit smoking and no one went on vacation together—certainly not his parents, who got divorced shortly after their 25th anniversary—she said her favorite thing about camping was the first cigarette in the morning.

"Go ahead, take one," she said quietly. Earl thought of lighting up one of her Kools, but he knew what she meant. His favorite thing about camping was the smell of bacon, the ground still wet with dew, the bite of cool morning air before the heat of the day. Crisp, everything crisp. He bit into a strip.

"There'll be other girls," his mother said.

"Yeah," he said slowly—chewing, crunching, swallowing.

"Have lots of girlfriends," she said. "Your father didn't, and look at him," she said. They heard a stirring in the Apache.

Earl laughed because he didn't know what else to do. What she didn't say was, look at me.

"I mean it," she said. "Have another slice."

———————

"Your kiss tastes like bacon," Emma said.

"I hope it does," Earl said. "I used bacon mouthwash this morning. And bacon deodorant." He lifted his arm in Emma's face. She laughed.

"But you didn't notice my bacon perfume," she said. Earl leaned over and kissed her neck, losing himself in her long dark hair.

"Tastes like rattlesnake," he said.

"They always say rattlesnake tastes like chicken," she said.

"Not you," he said. "You taste like rattlesnake and . . ." He almost said "I love you," but that seemed too crazy.

———————

Earl was putt-putting by himself on the felt-covered course next to the snack bar. He'd just smoked half his second joint on one of the nature trails that no one ever hiked because they led you in a big circle through a hot, swampy, buggy open field behind the lake.

The mini-golf course was state-of-the-art, worthy of the upscale Timber Shores logo: a waterfall, a castle, a windmill—all the finer putt-putt features. A family of four was dawdling in front of him, and Earl was waiting for an opportunity to play through when he felt a hammy Buckeye fist on his shoulder: Rolfe. He shuddered.

"Son," he said. "I don't think it's true that you're a born-again cussing homo Christian. That just doesn't make any sense."

"Aw, I was just making stuff up," Earl said to Rolfe, trying to shake off the meaty hand and pull himself together.

"The kids feel like you're pissing on the whole Buckeye nation," Rolfe said.

"I don't think Peggy and Beau care much about anything I say," Earl said.

"You should see ol' Beau ski," Rolfe said.

"How is he *ol'* already? Is his name really Beau? I mean, c'mon—that's the kind of name they invent for TV."

"Irish name I think. All I know is that boy's a fucking natural on skis. Not like some asshole I remember from last year."

Fuck? Earl jerked his head back as if stung on the brain by a mad Buckeye bee.

"I was a fish out of water in the water," he said.

"Don't go talking Zen shit to me now, boy. You think I'm some dumb fuck from Ohio, but how do you think I can afford the boat, the trailer, all that?"

"Fuck?" Earl said aloud.

"I figure you ain't dating my girl no more, so I can just talk normal." Rolfe shrugged. "Specially after how you talked to poor Fat Becca. I know you know what I'm saying," he raised his already-loud voice. "Now . . . the point is, don't go upsetting our Buckeye girls. Plenty of white-trash Michigan girls out here might suit your style a little more."

"My style?" Earl leaned on his purple putter. He squeezed his purple ball in his sweaty hand. "I think you're taking this whole Ohio–Michigan thing a bit far. After all, what state are we in?"

"Don't think I didn't read all those dull-ass letters you sent. My gas bill was more entertaining reading."

Rolfe had the kind of look on his face Father Davenport had when he kicked Earl out of St. Michael's in eighth grade right before he was supposed to graduate. Earl'd set a bunch of paper towels on fire in the boy's room trash barrel, and even though he quickly extinguished it, the smell wafted out and clung to the hallways.

Rolfe's hair was cut into the flat scape of a perfect lawn. He had a Marine tattoo on one arm, and a Buckeye tattoo on the other. "Besides, this is a resort campground," Earl said. "No white trash here." It was all he could think to say. He was failing even at what he was good at—being a wise guy.

He putted a hole-in-one. Rolfe laughed. "Not bad for a shitty-ass Wolverine who can't ski or kiss. I hear you got a lottery ticket for me."

"Oh, I ripped that up, sir." Earl was suddenly tired. "Not a happy camper when I got here. You gotta understand . . ." Rolfe seemed to be growing into grizzly-bear proportions, or maybe it was just his shadow covering the green carpet in front of the tiny moat. Earl was waiting for the drawbridge to come down before he putted on the next hole.

Rolfe shook his head again. "Got a lot to learn, boy, and a campground in Michigan is not the place to learn it . . ." he paused and ran a meaty hand through his perfect lawn. He started away, then turned. "Me and you coulda been millionaires. . . ."

Earl watched him head toward the grownup Tiki Bar.

Peggy had relayed no message after Ohio State had won The Game again in November on yet another missed field goal by Michigan. Maybe Earl should've taken it as a sign. Maybe Rolfe was right about that learning thing.

———————

Beau gave Peggy a big old hickie on the neck—no hiding it at a beach campground. This pissed off Ralph/Rolfe. Peggy got grounded on the Shores of Timber. Bummer. The entire Buckeye Nation seemed to be mourning their golden girl. One purple mark on one sweet neck was creating a cluster-fuck in 45. Earl peered through the trees and watched Becca, red-eyed and somber, play Go Fish with little Buckeyes. He took little satisfaction. Truth was, he'd never given or received a hickie. Maybe you had to ask—he wasn't sure how that all went down.

———————

"I bet you buried it," Emma said. "I hope you didn't smoke it all already," she said, putting her arm through Earl's. "I think everyone going to that dance has cooties," she said. "Don't you hate the word *teen*? It's like a code word for cute and well-behaved, like our parents want. Like the name of some soap that turns you into a boring person. Have you ever been to this place before? I wanted to stay home—I got a job at Dairy Queen in East Detroit—East Pointe now, like getting rid of Detroit would make it less 'Detroit,' right?" She inhaled, paused to breathe. She pretended to elbow him in the ribs with an endearing exaggerated gesture. "So, hey, where you from, and what is your secret name?"

"Off Eight Mile, the Warren side," he said. "I like how they added that E onto Pointe to make sure we got the point." Earl felt like a sweet dark angel had alit from the sunset over Lake Michigan. He squeezed her arm against his side. "Are you a dark angel of the sunset?" he asked.

"You are stoned," she said. "You staying here all week? I've never been camping—what do you do besides lose all your privacy?"

He laughed. "Yeah, I'll be here. I was going to spend it spying on my old girlfriend from Ohio, but hanging out with you seems like a better plan."

"Oh, it most definitely is," she said, skipping down the dirt road in front of him into darkness. The skipping had a carefree purity, a different innocence than the Buckeyes had—a further-back kind that had nothing to do with wholesomeness. When they got to Cluster 39, Earl slipped in the Apache and grabbed his radio. In the dim campfire light in the distance, he saw Vince leaning into his father, Alice on his mother's lap, all of them huddled together, a clump on the edge of a cluster. He shook off a hollow chill and hurried back to Emma.

They smoked a joint down by the lake. He was glad his pot was quality stuff. Jerry had a connection—one of the guys at the Hi Fi station next to the Last Stoppe. They watched the teens spill out of the dance in ragged, bouncing groups in the distance. "This whole cluster thing—it's like some kind of board game come to life," she said.

Her name was Emma DeYoungs, and she did not care about Buckeyes and Wolverines. She went to as many rock concerts as she could afford at Masonic Temple and the Grande Ballroom and the big arena shows at Cobo. They'd gotten stoned and lost hearing simultaneously at many of the same shows. As they recounted their shared history, the music seemed to ring in his ears in the eerie quiet of that calm lakeshore.

Emma kissed him hard on the mouth when they parted. "Promise me we're gonna get through this week," she whispered into his shoulder, then walked down into her Cluster 23. She clearly didn't want him seeing or being seen by whatever family awaited her—he hadn't asked. She was stuck going up to Mackinac Island the next day. "I know where you live!" she turned and shouted. "I'll find you when I get back!" He smiled up at stars they never saw in Detroit. He didn't know if they had enough pot to last or if it mattered. Having to spend a day without her made Earl anxious—vacation time both speeded up and slowed down normal time.

He saw the glow of two cigarettes in the canvas folding chairs outside the Apache.

"Did you dance?" his mother asked. The other kids were asleep. His father snorted.

"It was the Land of 1000 Dances," he said, then slipped into the camper.

"Don't forget to brush your teeth," his mother said, but he crawled into his sleeping bag and was gone.

———————

"Hey, dude," Beau said. Earl was putt-putting stoned again.

"Can't a man putt-putt in peace in this place?" Earl complained, looking up from the windmill hole.

"Earl, yah?" Beau stuck out his hand. He carried himself with a rural confidence that seemed foreign, along with the strange lilt of his Yooper accent.

"Beau, right?" Earl awkwardly shook hands while holding the putter. "Watch me ace this baby."

Earl measured his putt while Beau watched patiently. The ball rolled straight through the turning windmill and into the hole.

"Dude," Beau said again. "Free game." Earl did an exaggerated strut to the hole to retrieve his striped purple ball.

"Dude, I heard you were bummed about me and Peggy, eh? I didn't know about last summer."

"Dude," Earl said, bent over his putter like an old man with a crutch. "It was just a campground thing."

"Cool. But Ralph told me about the lottery ticket. You shouldn't be ripping up stuff over a campground thing."

"I thought it was Rolfe?"

"Dude, it's the Ohio accent I think."

"Buckeye Nation," Earl said, banking a shot that lipped the hole on its way out of the tunnel. "Speaking of accents, you got the whole Yooper thing going."

"Menominee, yah. Those girls love it, eh. Anyway, no hard feelings, dude. Those people are all in some kind of cult."

"Next year, they're all gonna show up here with shaved heads and Hare Krishna robes."

"What's that?"

"Ah, never mind, Beau. Beau," Earl giggled. "We're cool." They shook hands. "Wait a sec."

Earl ran to the booth and got his Free Game ticket and gave it to Beau. "Here. Don't rip it up."

———————————

Earl could not sing around a campfire. No hippies with guitars in sight. In all those clusters, not one hip campfire. He and Emma cruised them all. They smoked the rest of his pot on Wednesday. On Thursday, she gave him a wicked smile, then pulled out her own little baggie.

"Holding out on me?" Earl said, half-hurt, half-glad.

She hung her arms around his neck. They were walking in the cool night sand on the edge of the lake. Small waves lapped against their bare feet.

"Yeah, I guess I was," she said. "That first night I was being a moocher. Then, I didn't want you feeling like you're feeling now. Hoping you'd like me enough later to forgive me," she tilted her head and gave him a crooked smile. She dangled the baggie in the air.

"What do you say, Earl, old pal, old chum?"

Earl and Emma settled on a retiree fire in Cluster 1 on their final night together. The end of a camping trip was always sad, whether you'd had a miserable time or a great time.

The retirees belonged to a caravan club near Chicago and filled their cluster for a month every summer. They had upholstered camp chairs and identical Airstream trailers. Due to either the length of their stay of the length of their lives, they didn't seem to expect much from a campground, quietly and politely circling their modest fire.

"Hi, we're from East Pointe, Michigan," Emma said, poking Earl in the ribs. He was happy to be part of a "we," a small joke for themselves. They settled on the ground close to the flames. Everyone nodded and acknowledged them, then carried on as if they were invisible. It was almost perfect. Until one of Earl's sneakers began to melt in the heat. The retirees thought that was hilarious. He ran off with his hot foot, and Emma ran after him, laughing and gasping.

They lay together, sprawled in the sand. Chilly away from the campfire, no towel beneath them, wind swooping in off the lake. He nudged himself closer. "Can you give me a hickie?" he asked.

She laughed. "A hickie? I'll give you a damn blow job."

Earl burst out with an odd choking eruption of surprise that rolled her over into laughter. He clutched her soft, tender belly.

"Just kidding," she said—soft, sudden, serious. She touched his forehead as if taking his temperature. "Maybe back in Detroit," she said.

"Some day. We can get a hotel room—go completely crazy." She stretched out the *crazy*. It dissipated in the breeze. She curled back into him, but Earl felt a new chill. He wondered if he'd even see her in Detroit. Their letters could reach each other quicker. Hell, they could even talk on the phone without long distance charges. But what would they say?

When Earl returned to Eight Mile, and his job at the Last Stoppe, Jerry asked, "Did you get it on with that chick from Cleveland?"

"No, I did not," Earl said, trying to sound casual. Despite the optimistic placement of the rubber in the hidden compartment of his plastic wallet, he had not gotten it on with anyone. Not the rock goddess Emma DeYoungs.

"That girl turned out to be a square," Earl said. "She thought CKLW was a *Cleveland* station, and she likes Tommy James and the *Shondells*."

"He's from Niles, Michigan," Jerry said.

"Yeah, but he still sucks," Earl said. "I did meet a rock goddess from East Detroit though."

"It's East Pointe now," Jerry said. "So, did you bang her?" Jerry was a grungy stoner with poor personal hygiene. Earl suspected he had not "banged" anyone.

Earl's parents had seen him holding Emma's hand. Vince told him his father called her "that hippie girl." Their father had stepped up and taken charge of the cluster's campfire by arriving early, before dark. Teepee method, one match.

"She's Emmma with three m's," Earl told Vince. "But don't tell anyone—it's a secret m." Vince was crunching the chocolate-covered bees he'd purchased at some tourist trap on the first rainy day of the week. It sounded like Vince said "that chippie," but Earl didn't think his dad would ever say chippie.

"The world is made of more than Buckeyes and Wolverines," Earl told Vince, a speedy running back on his Pee Wee Football team, despite sucking at tetherball.

"Words of wisdom from the man with the radio," Vince said. He was short for his age and thus was already developing a quick wit as a layer of insulation against teasing and insults, like he was a sports announcer narrating their lives—an observer of all things, but of Earl in particular. "What do the Martians think?"

———————

On the beach, in the rain, Emma and Earl got soaked. If it was a movie, they would have gone somewhere to dump their wet clothes and have sex, but Timber Shores had no Teen Sex Salon, and though the pop-up camper was empty, it had no back door, and Earl had no idea when his parents would return, given his father's dread of shopping. Their loathing of souvenir shoppes seemed to be the only thing Earl and his father shared, which made it hard to bond the other 51 weeks of the year.

The last time they'd gone out for souvenirs together, they were camping at Pinery Provincial Park in Canada and ended up smuggling a brick of firecrackers back over the border, so their mother no longer trusted them. Their father let the kids buy anything just to get out of those fake Indian shops that sold rubber tomahawks and feathered headdresses, or the potpourri places with fragile merchandise that they might break and have to pay for. One year he and Vince got rawhide whips that their parents had to take away after a little accident in the backyard.

———————

"C'mon, Earl," his mother had urged. "This might be our last vacation as a family."

"You want me to be miserable on our last vacation?" he asked.

"You're always miserable, Earl," Vince piped in, already in the back seat of the car, buckled up, ready to go: *he* wasn't missing out on souvenirs.

His mother stifled a laugh. Earl sat on the wet picnic table and felt water seep through the butt of his jeans.

"Let him stay, Ann," Leroy said. It looked like he was going to say more, but he just repeated, "Let him stay," softer, resigned, then he jingled his keys and turned away, getting in the station wagon and starting it up. His mother shrugged at Earl in a sad, exaggerated way. Large raindrops suddenly spattered on the table. She stood under a piece of the old tent his father had staked up as a makeshift porch for the Apache. Rain drummed off the canvas and rattled the metal roof of the Apache like cymbals. Was his mother crying, or was it rain? She also looked like she wanted to say something, but she also turned away and got in. Vince made a face at Earl through the car window. Silent Alice glared out at him, accusatory and grim. Alice, the last child. Where would Earl be when she was his age?

Earl remembered camping in their old tent in the rain. They'd all lay on their sleeping bags like the points of a star with their heads in the middle, resting on elbows as their father dumped out wooden matchsticks they used as chips in high-stakes poker games without stakes—anteing up to pass the time. Alice curled into a nap beside them. Thinking about the simple peace of sleeping in a tent in the rain nearly choked Earl up. They always had a deck of cards, and sometimes it was all they needed. No antennas. No joints.

At Timber Shores, Earl realized he needed sunglasses. Every other teenager had them. Even the Buckeyes. Emma wore mirrored granny glasses she'd found at a head shop down on Plum Street, Detroit's tiny hippie enclave Earl'd never been to—he could get rolling papers at Max's.

He needed cool sunglasses to go with his cool radio. In another year, he'd be driving and need shades for cruising. If he'd had to go souvenir shopping, he would've been twirling the racks of sunglasses in order to be ready once the skies cleared.

————————

Earl watched through the shelter of trees as his father smoked cigarette after cigarette in his lawn chair in the patch of grass in front of the Apache. His heart hollowed out into reverb—he rarely got to watch his father do anything, much less observe him secretly. Back home, his father was either at work, in bed, or watching TV in their tiny living room. This was his father's one week away from home, and he'd let Earl lead them back to Timber Shores on the vague promise of a girlfriend, the sickly sweet pink envelopes that arrived from Cleveland addressed to Earl that his father or mother handed over, perhaps with a slight smile. Though any smile from his father was rare, and not slight.

————————

"Emma, I need cool sunglasses," he said. They were sprawled on the outer edge of the crowded beach near where weeds took over and someone else's shores began. He squinted over at her lying on her ratty Keep On Truckin' towel.

"The sun never shines in Detroit," she said. "At least when I'm up. But yeah, you could use some cool shades. Go down to Plum Street. They have cool posters too. I got a black-light Hendrix one. I'm saving money for a black light."

"I've got a black light," he said, "but no posters. I found it garbage picking, and it still works."

"How can you tell?"

"My underwear glows," he said.

Her long purple-nailed fingers brushed his face in a caress.

"We can live together, your poster, my black light."

"We can have little concerts in our basement," she said. "We'll grow our own pot under grow-lights."

"No fucking teen dances for us."

"We'll have pancakes and bacon for breakfast every day."

"My mom makes great bacon. We can invite her over."

"We can light one up with Moms and watch the walls glow."

Earl felt the sun through his closed eyelids. He picked up her glow-in-the-dark Frisbee, knowing it had rested against her small butt. He tossed it gently upward, then caught it. It was as real as any future he could imagine. Warm sand slipped through his fingers. He giggled. "Moms," he said. "Here, take a hit."

Emma giggled too. She reached across and took his hand, and they were briefly anchored to a future without complication or consequence. The storm coming in off the lake could go fuck itself.

———————

His father had offered to give him a driving lesson on inland back roads that crisscrossed cherry orchards. Raining again, and Earl had already spent two dollars in quarters at the pinball machine in the Teen Center. He returned to the campsite half-soaked and slipped under the tarp.

"Dad," he said, Can we try driving today?"

"Can we?" his father laughed. "Sure, we can."

They dropped the others off for more souvenir shopping. Vince had his eye on a corncob pipe. Alice wanted a Petoskey stone, since she'd been unable to find one on the beach. His father turned inland off the state highway and found a long, straight gravel road. He put the car in park and switched places with Earl.

———————

Emma was at Indian River visiting the world's largest wooden crucifix. Her mother's new boyfriend seemed to have a thing for Emma—enough for her to worry, to sleep tight against her mother in their rented trailer, finding refuge in her old enemy to avoid the new. "Can you think of anything I'd like to see less?" Emma asked him, a Catholic school reject like

Earl. She mimed hanging on the cross to make him laugh. She slumped further. He laughed harder.

"Do they have an elevator to the top?" he asked.

"No, but if you stay there three days, you can rise from the dead."

"Been there, done that," he said.

"Having a wonderful time. Wish you were there." She shrugged, then gave him a quick hug and ran off into the dark, knotted cluster where they waited for her.

He felt as nervous as when he'd tried to water ski, though there was nowhere to fall except into shallow roadside ditches.

"Can I turn on the radio?" Earl asked.

"No," his father barked. "Jesus, Earl, I'm trying to teach you something. God knows you already know how to operate a radio."

Earl lifted his foot off the brake, then jerked the steering wheel back and forth across the road as the car chugged along, wipers whupping back and forth. He gave it enough gas to jolt the lumbering wagon ahead, then he hit the brake again. His father jerked forward, then leaned back and blew smoke out the corner of his mouth.

"If the whole world drove this slow," his father said, "maybe it'd be a better place. Or maybe just more boring. What do you think, son?"

"Don't grip the wheel so tight," his father said, so Earl didn't have to answer. His father rarely called him son. *Son.* The word stabbed Earl in the gut.

"Damn it, give it some gas."

The wagon stalled at a crossroads and blocked traffic. Earl was flooding the engine. Cars appeared out of nowhere to accumulate behind them, honking their horns.

"Oh, hell," his father said. "Move over." Earl slid across the bench seat, and his father got out and jumped in the driver's side. "Student driver," he shouted, waving to the angry cars on all sides. "Not quite ready," he chuckled madly, shoving Earl over further.

They picked up the others at the Mohawk Souvenir Shoppe. Everyone seemed happy as they got back in the car. Alice wore a tiny headdress and clutched her stone. Vince wore a new, beaded belt and clutched a tiny pipe between his teeth.

"I yam what I yam and dats what I am!" he shouted.

"So, how'd it go?" their mother asked hopefully.

"Rome wasn't built in a day," their father said, turning to Earl, "right, son?"

"That's what they say on TV," Earl said. Vince poked him with his pipe.

"You, driving a car," he said, and laughed.

"Dad won't let you smoke it," Earl said.

"Who cares," Vince said, and poked him again.

Emma and Earl pasted themselves against each other, and Earl learned another wonderful thing about rain—that kissing in it can be pretty amazing—warm mouths hot against it, everything wet, slippery, cold, warm. Until they got chilled and could not get unchilled. Emma's teeth began chattering. Earl remembered his water-skiing numbness. He desperately wanted to make her warm, but that would involve removing their clothes and creating friction, and they had no place to stoke that kind of fire. Nothing dries quickly when camping in rain in Northern Michigan in the shadows of pines, but oh, the sweet, wet smell.

They gave each other shotguns with the last joint. When they weren't stoned, they were shy. They kissed slow and sensuous in the mixed smells of pot and pine. Emma had only an old baggy blue one-piece suit—East Detroit/Pointe did not have a city pool. She wore a T-shirt over the suit while they sat in the sand and listened to the music of each other's concerts in their heads. Earl loved that plain suit in bikini land, the opposite of Peggy's look-at-me suit she was busting out of. Back in Shaker Heights, Peggy would be part of the popular crowd. She would cheer at the pep rallies and make locker posters for athletes. The elastic on his own faded brown suit was worn, and when he dove into the water, he had to quickly yank it up over his ass crack.

Emma was staying at Timber Shores with her mother and a man who claimed to be her soon-to-be stepfather, and she had to join them in their rented trailer for meals. Why would anyone *rent* a trailer? Earl imagined it cost as much as a week in a hotel. Emma thought the whole trip was a tryout for a potential new family, and she didn't want to make the team. She felt like she was interrupting something whenever she showed up at the trailer. They focused their lasers on her. "It's like they're quizzing me on something, but I don't know what. I don't have the right answers."

"Three's a crowd," Earl said.

"You don't know a thing about it," she said. "And I'm not even going to get into my father's story. Your family seems pretty normal."

"Sorry," he said. He placed his hands on her small hipbones and wondered if she was too thin. He nudged his forehead into hers and felt a light sweat beading beneath her hairline.

"I'm a little jealous," she whispered.

Walking in the rain had seemed like a good idea, but Earl was beginning to realize that he got a lot of his ideas from bad TV. He watched on the old black-and-white in their basement while their mother dealt with Vince and Alice upstairs. Their father rarely made it home in time to see them awake. The TV lulled Earl to sleep as he sprawled on the Danish Modern couch that they took from their grandmother's when she died.

It smelled like her. She was the first person Earl knew who died. He liked to sleep on it and imagine she was still around.

Since neither of them could drive yet, and talking on the phone was inadequate and not private in either of their houses, Earl and Emma exchanged addresses and wrote letters. Emma wrote hers on black paper with silver ink, and despite many misspellings as she detailed how much she'd partied and how bored she was, Earl loved those letters. They did not need to be spelled correctly or make any sense. They had a smell to them—not bubble gum like Peggy's. Earl's mother could not identify the smell, which he later learned was patchouli. Black paper. Silver ink.

He imagined trying to use their phone in the kitchen with Vince staring at him, waiting to be entertained, mimicking him clutching the receiver. The distance from Earl's house on the edge of Detroit to Emma's in East Pointe was less than ten miles—he could have probably walked there if he'd had a decent pair of sneakers and a good map, but he had neither. The school and his burnout friends and the party store soon weighed him down, like before.

Emma hated school. Her soon-to-be stepfather tried to come on to her one night, as predicted and feared. Her mother said she'd misunderstood. She wanted to run away with Earl, who'd gotten a speeding ticket and lost his license for six months just three weeks after getting it. *Run away*. He trembled, reading those words in her sure, silver script.

His father lied at the hearing, saying Earl needed the car for work. It was something he could do for his son. Like Timber Shores. If he ran away with Emma, there'd be no help coming.

Earl ventured down to Plum Street and got a pair of mirrored sunglasses to surprise Emma when he saw her again. She would smile and laugh. He could see it already. He felt for sure this lottery ticket would pay off.

When Earl listened to WABX, he knew Emma was listening. They both knew where CKLW was from—they'd both been in that other country and handled its odd-colored currency adorned with the placid face of the queen. Earl could not help anticipating seeing Emma again, despite having learned the lesson of water-skiing long distance and pretending to be someone else. Earl was not a runner, not a skipper. He was a stoner. He dreamed of surprising her at work at the Dairy Queen once he got his license back, but when spring came, the letters stopped.

───────────

He did see her again—he was sure of it—at a concert at Masonic Temple by New Riders of the Purple Sage, and Commander Cody and His Lost Planet Airmen. During the drum solo, the Commander and the other lost airmen wandered off stage, and the bathrooms had filled with partying stoners. Emma had barged into the raucous men's room to pee—a not uncommon concert occurrence when the women's room line snaked down the long curved hallways—she was drunk, stoned or both, shouting at her girlfriend, a partner in their daring incursion.

"Are you fucking crazy?" Emma said. Earl was standing at a urinal. He turned his head, but she'd hurried into a stall with her friend where they were screeching and laughing and apparently peeing. Earl zipped up fast and turned around to surprise her, but when the girls burst out of the stall, Emma's friend bumped right into Earl and said, "Hey, who the fuck are you?" And Emma said, "Yeah, who the fuck are you?"

Some of other guys in the rowdy room got semi-quiet, staring at Earl. She had hardly given him a glance, and off they staggered out the open door. "Emma," he quickly turned and shouted after them, but they did not turn around. A crowded bathroom full of stoners—his people. Who the fuck *was* he?

Context is everything, he might tell his brother Vince some day.

Who wrote the last letter was hard to tell—they crossed paths in the mail. She ran out of silver ink in the middle of hers and wrote the rest in blue—she must've taken it as a sign. Her *Emma*, barely legible, blue against black, missing at least one *m*.

Goodbye, goodbye, goodbye, Earl practiced. He felt sorry for Peggy. Particularly after Beau gave a hickie to *another* girl at the End-of-the-Week Shiver Me Timbers Teen Dance—that man was a hickie machine. Watching the trailers leave on Saturday, Earl saw Beau coolly observing from a distance as they pulled up one by one to the wooden exit gate, many of them stopping at the dumping station to unload the week. New trailers pulled in on the other side, checking in.

He'd wanted to say "No hard feelings" to Peggy—she had done nothing except be a cute fifteen-year-old girl who filled out a bikini better than most. Who could've expected her to wait a whole week for Earl to show up? A whole week in Timber Shores time?

He had built his bridges and burned them too. He had blown them up like over the River Kwai, though he didn't even know how to whistle or whittle. He doubted the Buckeye Nation would let bygones be sleeping dogs. He wasn't even sure they noticed he'd been avoiding them.

Earl took a last walk through the campground after smooching with Emma in daylight while she waited for the future stepfather to come back with the car from parts unknown and hitch it up to the trailer. When he spotted Rolfe lowering his own trailer onto the hitch of his *Go Buckeye* pickup truck, he shouted, "I set my shoes on fire last night!" His wife Red idled in another pickup that pulled the speedboat. Peggy sat in the passenger seat, her beautiful blonde hair plastered against the window. From where he stood, she looked like a carsick dog. Rolfe shooed in his direction as if swatting a fly. Just then, Vince yanked on Earl's jeans—their father wanted him to help uncrank the Apache.

Back in Warren, Earl sat in his underwear with the black light on and put joints in the battery compartment of his radio again so he could tune in the static of those two weeks, a year apart, at Timber Shores. Though no one would call it music, Earl hummed along to memory-glow like a half-forgotten prayer from back when he still believed. The problem was, the words and days got mixed up in the weak signal from his bent antenna.

"I don't want to be a stoner," Earl told his mother.
    "Oh, honey," she said.

Alone in the basement, Earl wrote a thank-you note to his parents for returning to Timber Shores for the second year. He was saving the letters from both Peggy and Emma. He wasn't sure why. Perhaps as evidence. Proof of something about himself separate from Jerry at Max's, from Ellen at Valu Time. Receipts for secrets, not souvenirs. Some day, he would no longer need them, but he needed them now. Stacked, rubber banded, hidden under one of the Velcro-ed speaker covers from his stereo.

    He took a stamp from the roll in the closet next to his parents' cartons of cigarettes and the box of church envelopes. On the way to school the next day, he dropped the note in the mailbox at the corner.

Everyone knew there'd be no third year. His parents never said a word about the note, but that's the way it was in his family—even while it was falling apart, no one talked about how they really felt. You had to go outside and mail a letter to say anything like that.

"You're looking a gift horse in the house," Vince told him once. That sort of summed things up.

———————

The right answers. No one had the right answers for each other, Earl realized. No one was grading the tests, and everyone was grading the tests. Everyone was cheating, but cheating did not help. Teenagers and their parents, boys and girls. Earl wished he had the answer key for someone. Next summer, in his sunglasses, he'd be better at hiding everything, and what potential bribes could his parents have left? And who would teach him how to steer his life when it counted?

No one, he knew. No one.

———————

"How are those bees?" he asked his brother in the silent car on the long drive home.

"Try one," Vince said, pulling out the small package from his pocket. Earl knew it was a trick because they never shared anything with each other. He knew better, but still, he reached in and took one. Because there were no right answers. Earl bit down hard like it was a chewable vitamin. Like it was good for him.

Danish Modern

Angie and I started having sex in the basement—started and finished, started and finished, habitual favorite sin. I shared a bedroom down there with my little brother Vince. He wasn't home, but he might be soon—too young to find us naked in our room. We were better off around the corner on the old Danish Modern couch up on blocks due to broken legs. In Detroit, concrete blocks had many functions—for cars, couches, bookshelves. No, not bookshelves—part of a different life years away by car or hot-air balloon in a city named for the dawn. The couch's synthetic fibers scratched our skin—we covered it with a sheet in summer. Even in that dark basement, the heat dug in. We sweat our silhouettes into that sheet. We yanked it off the prickly cushions. I don't know what made that couch Danish or Modern. Short, so we angled our heads away from the wooden armrests. Armrests with caning. If we pressed into them, they gave a little. Not like a pillow, but almost enough. I lay on the bottom. We were used to wedging our hands down each other's pants—removing pants seemed entirely too much—they dangled around ankles. "Don't worry about little Vinnie," I said, "We'll hear him coming down." Our bedroom at the bottom of the stairs, with its clunky sliding door, a "gift" from the lumberyard where my Uncle Ted worked. Closing it announced a guillotine coming down. The couch faced the old TV we turned on when my parents were home to hide half-stifled moans evoked by wedged hands—but they were not home. "Ohio, Canada, I don't know where!" I shouted. "Gone!" Empty house! I strained one foot pushing the shoe off the other, tied tight that day of all days. From the bottom I looked into the rafters where I hid *Playboys* in my old wood burning kit. That dates me, the wood burning, the *Playboys*. Almost quaint now. Before *Penthouse* upped the ante by showing pubic hair. Pubic—such a strange, unromantic word. Close to public. We were private. I was sucking her sweet breasts while she bent forward on top of me. Her skin glistened with sweat and saliva as the sun filtered in through the basement casement windows. I never noticed that rhyme before. How could I not? My father wanted to glass-block them up, but I told him if we had a fire, we'd be trapped. Casement windows, we could crawl out of. *Playboys* and wood burning—who knew what could happen? He called me a sissy, but didn't block them up till we moved out. Every house, one story, and every street, flat—the sun snuck in at dusk down there. Everything safe and public happened in that one story. We had to go to the basement to find another, to kill crickets and spiders and mold. We had to be moles in the dark. I heard a car door slam. We both did. Were they back from Ohio? Our lips formed the O. Vince was ten. He would tell if he caught us. He didn't have pubes yet. I forgot to tell you, my grandmother's upstairs, but she's deaf and can no longer handle the steps. Dead, as far as the basement is concerned. The basement doesn't seem concerned. It's great to be fucking on Danish Modern with Angie who is so enthusiastic she will be pregnant within six months with somebody else's baby. I am wearing a condom. We called them rubbers. Some of us still do. Quaint too? Like putting a boot on it. All that shit's later though. The tears, the snot, the breakup. We came on it—tipped over cinder blocks with our rocking, and the couch crashed to the tile floor. It took my father five years to tile that cement. Don't look too close near the walls where he ran out of room. Maybe four years. It seemed forever. I sat on the steps watching him tile from that tilted island of exile. It was his Mt. Everest. I mean Rushmore. I mean Everest. Running out of room was the lesson. She fell, and I fell and fell out of her. Grandma upstairs may have felt a vibration. What about the car? I forgot about the car. Maybe our neighbor Mrs. Cooper out back. She always slammed the door hard. It sounded closer—it always does, I suppose, when you're fucking in a basement. We could never banish the mold. It grew on cement walls in the bedroom beneath cheap wood paneling installed by the Great Dad-Vinci. We lay on the floor on top of each other but not in each other, laughing wide-mouthed and insane, like we were going to puke if we didn't laugh harder— young and beautiful, our pants and underwear around our ankles—my grandmother might've cried to see us or slipped down our slippery sinner's steps—she'd taught my brother all about Jesus, and that shit was sticking to the little tattle-tale. I had to share the room with him and listen to his sanctimonious bedtime prayers, bless this and bless that. We started making love in the basement and never finished. We never fucked upstairs anywhere—I'm not counting car seats—also quaint. Maybe I never had a rubber and the couch was our lucky break. We got dressed and raised up the tumbled blocks—you can't break a cement block unless you're doing karate on TV—and balanced the Danish Modern back on top just as Vince was fumbling with the side door. I heard him unzipping his rubber boots on the stairs where we stacked them—each of us had a step. It must've been winter not summer if he wore boots, and cold in the basement, her nipples like sweet pebbles in my mouth—memory is shortsighted. Grandma couldn't drive anymore. That was mean, what I said earlier. She gave Angie a rose in the backyard one summer day while we sat in the grass during our early days of canoodling—the sweetest thing I'd ever not thought of myself—I wasn't good at sweetness, thinking about wood burning, erector sets, all the time—I mean erector sex all the time—little Vince coming down the stairs, and we were all fixed up right like fucking soldiers and marched up the stairs past him without a word and out the side door, and he'd tell what he was going to tell when they got back from their foreign country—I'd just have to listen to his bedtime prayers that night to hear if he asked God to bless me.

Pop Quiz

1.

Our desks rounded up like dogies. Chubbs, the hungover history teacher, fiddled with his pull-down maps as if they were the Dead Sea Scrolls. Angie. Sigh—half gasp, half cough. Across the room, slouched surly in her chair, staring her daring lasers at me, legs brazenly parted, short skirt. I'm squeezing my chewed-up blue ballpoint. Please take me seriously—you're all going, *C'mon*, like I've just farted or picked my nose. I looked then and I'd look now, the map of Mesopotamia, the ancient borders color-coded, the Pleistocene Epoch fossilized into a statue of a god somebody once knew the name of. I'm supposed to be explaining why I think the Romans built the ark out of pyramid stones, but I just stare. Cheap pen leaks onto my fingers. Empty sheet of paper. Stopped clock. Dusty chalkboard. Bulletin board of dead leaves and stapled orange construction paper. Scuffed brown tiles. *None of the above.*

2.

At forty-three, Angie, long legs still sleek, even if she's not wearing her plaid St. Mike's jumper and kneeling to see if cloth brushes the tile floor while an angry nun uncoils toward her like one of those stinky black snakes we lit on bored summer sidewalks. On the reunion's empty dance floor, she leans into her third husband, grinding to some CD she brought in from her car and forced the DJ to play. In eighth grade, we lit teachers' cigarette butts in their lounge on Saturdays, blowing smoke into long kisses. Somebody had to feed the lab mice on weekends. I'm staring. Tasting cold ash and her sassy mouth. She cuts me a glance. For her Demonstration Speech, she gave mouth-to-mouth to some poor boy whose hard-on poked up like an eager hand waving in the air, sure of the answer. Nobody's got the answer. So why not rim your eyes in dark blue and toss back another virgin Bloody Mary? Pregnant, she dropped out. I ask only about the skirts, and she explains how she unrolled them quick, tugged down, leaned forward till they touched.

Honor Society

"Hey Mother Fucker, you leave Angie alone, you hear?"

Earl looked up toward the voice echoing down the long, empty hallway of Eight Mile High. Hawk, with his slicked-back hair and pointy black boots, was headed Earl's way. Four o'clock—just released from detention. The few times Earl had detention, Hawk had been there too. He seemed to have his own desk staked out, surrounded by his greaser friends in the sullen silence of the big monitored room.

Earl had just stormed out of a National Honor Society meeting at which he'd dramatically resigned in protest of the annual slave auction fundraiser. It hadn't had the game-changing effect he'd hoped for—no one followed him out, though he'd paused at the door and looked around with his most damning, pleading look at the smartest kids in the school—they had their NHS I.D. cards to prove it—who would not meet his eyes.

He wanted to give a lot of room to Hawk, Angie's new boyfriend, so Earl veered toward the wall of lockers on his left. But Hawk veered to follow. He cut Earl off and rammed him up against the locker of Darryl Kralitz, football star, decorated with an elaborate pep club poster. Earl felt the thick glitter prick through his thin shirt as Hawk leaned into him. Earl, who played no sports, choosing instead to work at Max's party store, suddenly wished for some jocky friends to be backing him up.

"I haven't talked to her since we broke up. You can have her, man, she's all yours," Earl blurted out. Hawk tightened his grip on Earl's neck while he tried to decide if someone had just been insulted.

"I didn't . . ."

"You saying she's no good?"

"No, no. I just—hey, you remember me. I used to deliver the *Free Press* to your house. How's your old man doing? How's that crazy dog?"

Hawk loosened his grip and frowned, repeating, "You saying she's no good? You think you're too good for her, mother fucker?"

Earl, who'd felt brave and self-righteous just minutes earlier at the NHS meeting, was now simply at a loss.

"You want to step outside, mother fucker?"

"Well, I . . ."

"C'mon, mother fucker, let's go." Hawk began yanking him toward the row of doors at the end of C Wing. Earl was trying to remember Hawk's first name. He was just Hawk. Like *fuck*. Compact, dangerous. A tight mass of bulging muscle and grudge.

"Listen, Keith, it just didn't work out with me and Angie," Earl pleaded, hating himself for pleading as he tried to pull the other way. "I'm *glad* you two got together. I hope you live happily—"

"It's Ken," he said, stopping just steps from the doors. "The dog got hit by a car."

"Ken, yes, Ken." Earl thought briefly of pointing out that *his* name, on the other hand, was not Mother Fucker, but he didn't want to lose his chance to slip out of this unharmed. The hallway was deserted at this hour, and the parking lot would be too. Greasers always wanted an audience for fights. What was the point if they couldn't taunt and boast and do all that other greaser stuff? Hawk was genuinely upset, Earl realized. Looking for somebody to beat up in order to simplify a situation that seemed over his thick greaser head.

"Why's she still talk about you all the time?" Hawk loosened his grip, tightened it again, then let go.

Earl paused. "You got me there, Ken." Why *would* she still be talking about him? He wanted to ask what she was saying, but that could be part of what made Hawk mad. Earl had subtly eased back a couple of steps and was ready to make a mad dash down the hallway toward what passed for civilization.

"Just leave her alone. I'm warning you." Hawk gave him a little shove.

The newspaper cost ninety cents a week. Most customers gave him a dollar and let him keep the change. The Hawks had never let him keep the dime, even at the holidays. Their yard looked like Earl's yard, their house a mirror image of Earl's ramshackle house over on Jackson Street. They kept the dime because they were poor. The Hawks lived on Archangel Street near his friend Rita. Earl envied the celestial name—he could look up and imagine something else entirely while delivering papers on Archangel. Jackson had become Jackass, tiny little Jackass Street next to the slummy trailer park.

Earl turned and hurried down the hall in the other direction. "I'm warning you," Hawk shouted one more time. Earl guessed he wanted some response.

"Okay," he shouted back. That seemed to satisfy Hawk, who pushed open the C Wing doors and disappeared.

––––––––––––

I'm going to leave *everybody* alone, Earl thought. It wasn't worth it— he'd gotten his act together, started getting good grades, got in NHS, only to become the ninety-cent asshole at the slave auction.

His one claim to fame had been almost being a dead guy in a party store hold-up, and now it seemed like everyone had moved on from that except Jerry's family, since he was the one who died.

The first person named Earl to be inducted into the National Honor Society at Eight Mile High, and now that accomplishment was forever tainted. Born in Tennessee, where Earl was not an uncommon name, before his father moved the family north to take a job on the line at Chrysler's. Here, the name suggested a southern jackass who lived on Jackass Street. A Li'l Abner relation. To try and cheer Earl up, put things in perspective, his father said he knew somebody back in Tennessee named Baby Brother Wilson. His father's name was Leroy, so he had no perspective himself. No Leroys in NHS, or in their entire school. His full name was Earl Junior Rhodes. Junior? Clearly not an option. A family name, his parents had told him vaguely—though he found no previous Earl in their twisted, gnarly tree.

Earl walked out the front doors of the school, passing under the glare of the school enforcer, Assistant Principal Barker, who was locking up the now-empty study hall to keep studiers out after hours. Earl had homework, but he was going home without books again. The ninety-cent asshole. Why *had* he broken up with Angie? Six months together. Six months of kissing and groping. Even when they went to the movies, it was only to make out in the back. They couldn't keep their hands off of each other. *Why* had he broken up with Angie? Did he actually get tired of "getting some" when that was the stated ambition of nearly all the guys in the school, greaser, jock, or other?

As he headed down the cracked sidewalk in front of the Hi Fi station across Eight Mile, the sting of spilled gas hit him, a truck refilling their underground fuel tanks.

Like the acrid twitch of lust rising up, dangerous, invisible. He and Angie had nothing else in common besides that lust—Earl imagined himself a rebel artist type who would leave town, go to college, discuss intellectual topics with intellectual girls in berets and smoke enough dope to meet Jesus up close and personal. Angie was a baton twirler and member of the Future Homemakers of America. A match made in heaven, right?

Nineteen seventy-four, and Eight Mile High was a hop, skip, and a rock toss away from Detroit, the largest black community in the country, yet his school was still having a "fun" slave auction fundraiser. If he was honest with himself, he might admit that if he'd sold for more than ninety cents, he might have let it slide, but as Mirabelle Riviere handed over her spare change out of sheer mercy and led Earl away, he began to imagine real slaves, and real dread. His imagination failed.

"Hey Mother Fucker, leave Angie alone!"

Earl was thinking of the 10,000 other things he might have said to Hawk. He always thought of great responses hours or days later, his brain on some kind of tape delay. With Angie, he never thought of things to say later, since they didn't talk much to begin with.

He had chosen of his own volition to leave her alone, and he was damn proud of that, considering Angie had a body one could get completely lost in, curve after solid curve. She was the first girl to let Earl touch her, and besides that, she was nearly an albino with the ghostly pallor he was trying to acquire himself. She had been his, all his, and now she was Hawk's, all Hawk's, if only Hawk would accept his good fortune.

After their breakup, Angie continued to come in the Max's Last Stoppe to buy cigarettes for her mother. Earl tried to hide, but Helen, his Polish grandmother of a co-worker, cut him off, her thick bulk effectively blocking the narrow doorway into the back of the store. Helen was a tough old woman who'd worked in the store since before Earl was born—so long that some customers thought she was Max's wife. Her own husband Steve had only one arm, and Helen swore that she'd cut the other one off, but everyone knew it was a factory accident and that he was drinking up his disability checks. She wanted Earl to "deal with that girl, boy."

He thought his first serious breakup was going to be simple, though everybody else seemed to take for granted that they'd have to break up at least a couple more times before it'd stick. He thought not being a racist was going to be simple, though everybody else seemed to take for granted that he'd never get over it.

"Hey Junior, you look like you seen the ghost of some albino chick," his pal Jerry said. Jerry shared the stock boy duties with Earl at Max's Quik Last Stoppe Party Shoppe. "I before E except after C," Max always said when asked to explain the spelling. "It makes the people stop," he said. "At least once."

"Shift change at Max's," Jerry shouted, slam-dunking his soiled white apron in the round cardboard laundry barrel with one hand, and giving Earl a high five with his other. Earl worked the 4–12 Saturday night shift. The worst shift of the week in a party store, everybody picking up their Saturday night beverages of choice.

Jerry had seniority, so he got off earlier on Saturday. In his last year at Eight Mile, he had just completed an unsuccessful bid for a school board seat, a novelty act that had accumulated enough press and sound bites on local TV and radio to last a lifetime. He'd just been turned down by the only college he'd applied to, the Big U, University of Michigan, and planned to head down to Macomb County Community College—better known as "12 Mile High"—instead, the self-correcting system doing its job. When anyone from Eight Mile got into the Big U, it usually happened after a couple of years of probation at the community college to make up for everything the high school lacked. Ambition was one thing Jerry did not lack, which, in a short life, might be a good thing—no point playing it safe if you end up dead at eighteen.

Max's was the last beer store before I-75, which explained the rest of the name—so convenient for both quik sales and quik robberies that the C was unnecessary. Boozers and thieves zoomed off down the freeway and quickly got lost in no man's land. Despite numerous robberies over the years, no one had ever been caught.

Jerry had a gun, one he bought out of the trunk of a car in the Hi Fi lot next door one night. Max, who packed one himself, didn't mind. Helen, on the other hand, had emptied Jerry's bullets into her apron like a crazy old grouch swiping kids' balls that landed on his lawn.

"What are you gonna do when we're held up, throw the bullets at them?" Jerry asked.

"Hell, no, I'm gonna give 'em the money, Gerald, like I always do."

"That's why they keep comin' back," Jerry replied. Maybe "hero" was on his ambition list too.

"That's enough, Mr. Wannabe School Board honky."

"Helene, now, you're not gonna tell me you didn't vote for me, are you?" Jerry asked. He had claimed he was running on a lark, but he took the loss hard. He missed the attention. Helen called him Gerald because he called her Helene, or vice versa. They both called him Junior after seeing one of his pay stubs. "Wait, did you just call me a honky? Do you have any idea what a honky is?"

Earl had no interest in guns. No interest in fist fights. His father had been wounded in Korea, and Earl was happy to be carrying around a high number in the Vietnam Death lottery.

"Army takes anybody named Earl Junior, no questions asked," Jerry had told him.

Jerry had asthma, and so the Army did not get Jerry. It did not have to.

The floodlight outside the store still buzzed and glowed in dawn's gray light as Max pulled into the store's rutted gravel lot to open up. The daily bakery delivery from Oaza's in Hamtramck would be arriving soon. Earl stood smoking a cigarette while he waited, one foot up on the dented guardrail.

Max leaned his balding head against the smudged glass cluttered with stickers advertising discontinued beer and pop brands while he deactivated the alarm and opened the door.

He still owned the next-door house, but refused to live in it anymore due to the relative lack of safety on that stretch of busy border road still stained with the smoke of suspicion from the Detroit riots of 1967. Instead, he rented it to a succession of surly tenants he always ended up evicting.

Earl walked in the store for the first time since the shooting and saw new bulletproof Plexiglas walls cutting off the customers from the help. A mini revolving door on the front counter was now the only place where goods and money could exchange hands. He almost choked up. It was like a shrine for Jerry—he would have been wryly amused by the unwieldy revolving door for six-packs of beer.

He waited as Angie walked up to the bulletproof glass and pressed a hand against it. Who's the prisoner here, Earl almost asked. He hated the muffled sound created by the new barrier.

"Tell Hawk I'm leaving you alone, okay?" he said.

"He likes me a lot," Angie said sadly.

"Yeah, tell me about it," Earl said.

"What?"

"I said 'great'!"

Helen, filling up the cigarette rack, handed him a pack of Kools automatically without looking up. In Max's, you knew what everybody smoked and drank, and how much.

Earl placed the cigarettes on the revolving wheel and turned it around so Angie could retrieve them. She put the money on the wheel and spun it back.

"I think I still love you," Angie shouted. No one knew how loud you had to talk to be heard through the Plexiglas. She'd never before said she'd loved him. What was this 'still' stuff? Earl trembled as he made change and funneled it onto the metal tray. Helen hummed in an obvious way to let him know she was listening while she stuffed cigarette packs into slots by brand. Earl loved the old woman just a little bit.

"I was gonna buy you at the auction," Angie continued.

"Ninety cents," he said, and she nodded.

Earl turned to Helen. "Ninety cents, can you believe it?" he said to her. He hadn't told her about the auction. Jerry probably would have if he hadn't gotten himself killed.

"Mirabelle wears too much makeup," Angie said.

"You should tell her," Earl said. "I think she needs your fashion acumen." Angie ignored his random comments, as she always had, but with the new glass, Earl wasn't sure she'd even heard him. Angie wore the thickest mascara in the world to compensate for her remarkably pale everything and considered herself an expert on makeup. She was an oddball like Earl, and he was wondering why he'd broken up with her again.

"I still love you." She always seemed to be squinting, sensitive to light, or just the weight of all that mascara.

"With that magic hair, you're going to live forever," he said, not knowing what he meant. He circled the change around for her to pick up. There was no way for their hands to touch, and he felt both sad and relieved. She shook her head, and one tear splashed against the thick Plexiglass.

"I can't take this," Helen said, and barreled around behind the deli counter to vigorously slice something up.

"You still gonna work here, after, you know?"

What was he worth? What was one life worth?

"Jerry, man." Earl felt tears welling up in his own eyes. "Shit." He was going to make a joke about being bulletproof, but instead started quivering and blubbering right there in front of all the shelves of hard liquor.

"Get outta here and take a break." Helen had suddenly returned, a large Polish ham balanced in the firm grip of one of her meaty hands. She grabbed his arm with the other and pushed him toward the back door.

"Touch that girl. Nobody's gonna kill you."

Plexiglas stood between him and the rest of his life. Between trust and betrayal. He took off his apron and pushed open the back door and walked into the light. He peeked around the corner and walked down the gloomy alley between the narrow buildings.

Max wanted to take him to a shooting range. A cop at the station had offered to set something up. "I aim for their eyeballs," he said. Earl had this odd tremble in his trigger hand even when he was holding a fork, eating some picrogi Helen had slathered in butter on the hot plate in the back room.

Earl remembered standing up on the makeshift stage in the cafeteria and feeling like it was a gallows. He put his hands behind his back as if they were tied. Mr. Chubbs, faculty advisor for the NHS, was the auctioneer. Darryl Kralitz, football captain and cheerleader heartthrob, had gone for $32 two places in front of him. Even Mary Neal, in front of him in line, burdened with her ordinary name and lack of physical development, went for ten, purchased by her friends from the Future Homemakers.

It seemed as if Mr. Chubbs said "Earl" with a slight sneer, but Earl suspected nearly everyone of constructing quotation marks around his name. How much for "Earl" here?

Earl hesitated to raise his eyes and scan the crowd, but with quick glances he noticed it had thinned substantially after Darryl's big sale. None of his friends had even bothered to show up. Likely out in the parking lot getting stoned like every other day.

"Who'll give me fifty cents for 'Earl'?" shouted Mr. Lucas Chubbs, handling the microphone like every tipsy lounge singer in every bad old movie. He taught history. Earl thought that with a name like "Chubbs," he should have been helping him out, but he just sounded bored—only five more in line, and he was ready to be done with it, or else still coming down from the Darryl Kralitz high. Earl wasn't a big sweater, but he felt the sweat trickle down from his underarms to the sides of his belly. Someone from the school paper took a photo. He flinched and hunched his shoulders as if he'd been hit. Mug shot. If he hadn't gone and broken up with Angie just a couple of weeks prior, this would've been a lot easier. Earl hadn't bothered to work out a deal for someone to bid on him—standard practice, he'd realized during the auction's first hour.

"Fifty cents." It was Ellen Loretish, who later went on to become Sister Ellen. Earl had no idea what she was doing at the Slave Auction. Maybe she felt bad for her Valu Time comment to his mother about him being a stoner. If he didn't know better, Earl could have mistaken her for a substitute teacher in her plaid skirt and no-nonsense sweater. She was always volunteering to help the poor, help the aged, help the orphans— you name it. She had even befriended the mysterious class transvestite, Bill Jansen. Now, it was Earl getting the pity. Could it get any worse?

Then he spotted Mirabelle counting her change off to the side. She and Darryl Kralitz had also broken up a couple of weeks earlier. Another sympathy bidder—their breakup would've made headlines if their school had a gossip rag, unlike Earl's breakup with Angie. He would've had to pay to get that in the personals. "Ninety cents!" she shouted. A little loud, Earl thought, for such a low bid.

Clearly, no spirited counter bid was forthcoming, so Chubbs brought the gavel down.

Tradition held that the next day—and Earl was just beginning to learn what a loaded word tradition was—all the owners could have the slaves do their bidding. Just like real slaves! How fun! This included dressing them up in odd, embarrassing outfits—(particularly cross-dressing—too bad Bill Jansen didn't have the grades—or maybe he did but opted out), spraying shaving cream on their heads, making them stand on tables and sing silly songs. Earl stepped quickly down off the platform while Mirabelle handed over her loose change, including five pennies.

"Thanks," Earl said.

"Don't worry, I won't make you do anything."

Mirabelle did wear a lot of makeup. She resembled the classic dumb blonde, but underneath the tanned skin and luscious curves and caked makeup, Earl imagined she had a soul—where was Darryl Kralitz? Turning her into a cartoon in the locker room with the other jocks.

"I can carry your books or something," he mumbled.

"Pretty depressing, isn't it?" she said. He wished that she'd have him do something, something small like make him stay home from school the next day to avoid the entire spectacle.

Earl smiled painfully. "The only thing that could've made it worse was if I'd pissed my pants up there."

Mirabelle laughed and touched his arm. "You are free to go, young man," she said in her version of an authoritative voice.

Earl thanked her again, and looked for Saint Ellen, but she had gone on to choir practice or something. He'd have to thank her later. Her and Mirabelle, his unlikely new friends.

———————

It probably wasn't a great idea to put a beer store that close to the expressway—a number of swerving, screeching near-accidents punctuated the daily grind through the screen door. In addition to the neighborhood regulars, the store attracted "Last Stoppers" on their way south to a rock concert downtown at Cobo Hall, or headed up north to escape to a cabin or cottage on some lake or river—everybody wanting to get a last-minute head start on their partying.

Max occasionally referenced the bullet holes in the wall, but they were up near the ceiling, so they still seemed mostly theoretical. Aside from the Last Stoppers, Earl knew 90% of the people who walked in the door. The other 10%, mostly black, were watched carefully by Max, who refused to cash their checks, protesting that he wouldn't know where to find them if the checks bounced, as if the other side of Eight Mile had never been mapped.

———————

Earl met Angie in front of the store where they had a tiny six-pack of a parking lot. He felt exposed everywhere now and lingered in the shadow of the dented aluminum awning. The two skinny black guys who robbed the store might be coming back to the scene of the crime to eliminate witnesses, or Hawk might be driving by with his goon friends, looking for revenge.

Angie fell immediately into his arms. All he could do was wrap her up as he staggered backwards. He felt her soft breasts against his ribs. He felt the tremble in his gun hand.

"I'm sorry," he said. "Hawk, he . . ."

"Shhhh," she said. "I just broke up with him."

Earl tried to pull back, but she held on tight. "What?"

"He's too jealous. He's always mad. He grunts instead of saying yes or no."

"I want you, but I'm afraid," Earl said. "We mess around, then we never have anything to say to each other. That ain't right."

"We're talking right now," she said. He heard the cigarette pack crackle in her fist. "Do I embarrass you?" she asked.

Earl looked out over the trashy parking lot. That'd been Jerry's job—he'd hang out in the parking lot sweeping up every little scrap just to get some fresh air and bullshit with the customers. And buy a gun. Why'd he do that? Earl wondered. Everything he did played at being a grown-up—the politics, the gun, the big talk—when Jerry would've been perfectly happy to some day buy the place from Max. He'd already acted like he owned it.

The drama of the funeral was over for the rest of the school. Bells rang, papers were turned in, or not. Tests were passed or failed. Kisses and punches were exchanged. Everyone went home, lived on, watched bad TV like it was the voice of God. Recited the prayers of their favorite songs. Genuflected at nothing.

Earl'd seen his friend bleed to death on Max's tile floor worn bare in front of the coolers from long years of lingering over choices. Yet he was the ninety-cent asshole. The one afraid to fight Ken Hawk. "Hey," he wanted to say. "Everyone who's seen somebody die, raise their hand. Now keep that hand up for the rest of your fucking life."

The robbery had obliterated his memory. The only thing he knew was that the robbers were black and had guns. "I coulda told you that, and I wasn't even there," a cop at the station said. The casual racism of the school, the store, the cops, widened the river of Eight Mile into an ocean. Earl could only peer across and squint at the other side.

"I think there's a lesson for you in this," Chubbs said when Earl spoke out at the NHS meeting. "Being smart does not make one popular."

Earl felt his knees wobble. It was like Chubbs was breaking up with him when he wanted to be the one doing the breaking up. He wanted to tell Chubbs he didn't think that was the lesson. That seeing somebody die was the lesson he was focusing on these days.

"It's about slavery," Earl said. "Slavery's not some joke." He emphasized *joke* a little louder than he meant to, as if hurrying to blurt it out to keep from crying.

Every single student, every single teacher and maintenance worker and bus driver. Everyone white. Earl had never thought that through before.

Just the way it was in Warren. It took a black man pointing a gun at him to realize it. He had a reason to hate a black man now, when before, he didn't need a reason. Just the way it was in Warren. At Eight Mile, the robbery seemed to have simply confirmed all the suspicion and distrust.

Earl flipped through the Book of Earl with fierce concentration while also flipping the pages of the mug shot books laminated to keep his fingerprints off the other fingerprints. Everybody in those books looked pissed off or stoned. They had entire books of black faces, though Warren had no black faces. The police fingerprinted him, then let him go, a useless witness. At night in bed, he fell asleep imagining flipping through those pages—a little sticky, some kind of human film coating them with germs he was not immunized against.

_____

"I'm a history teacher," Chubbs blanched. "I know about slavery."

"What's the lesson of the slave auction? Why can't we have a car wash, a bake sale?"

"I'm sorry if it was humiliating . . . to you," Chubbs said. "It's a tradition. No one's ever complained before, Earl."

"Do you? What do you know?" Earl sputtered. He wanted to say it was not about him, but of course it was.

Though the officers and other new members of the NHS sat squirming impatiently in Room 217, no one else spoke. Not Sliver Wrobleski, who had actually sold for 35 cents, the record low. Not Christine Yakamoto, whose grandparents had been rounded up during World War II. They had their fancy laminated I.D. cards, and they weren't going to give them up. Their parents were proud.

"After what happened to Jerry, now's not the time to be getting all self-righteous," Darryl Kralitz finally said, slouched in his desk, showing off his latest hickie as he stretched his neck back.

"That's got nothing to do with it!" Earl shouted. He knew he should have said more, but he did not. All these sudden blotches in his life bled into each other, blurring any clarity. He thought of many things to say later, too late. Earl stormed out of the room. He did not even officially quit. He abandoned the NHS, like he'd abandoned Angie, the church, his short-lived basketball career. He was becoming an abandoner.

———————————

In the yearbook, Darryl stands in the cafeteria wearing a dress, a colander on his head, whipped cream on his face. He appears to be singing a song. Maybe whistling Dixie, Earl thinks, flipping the page. Some days, he thinks he will tell his children all this. "When I was fifteen," he will begin, but he cannot think of what comes next.

To be bought and sold. Earl did not have the imagination for it. He didn't understand how it had existed for real in his country. To *own* another human being like a bicycle or stereo. Nobody called them "Negroes" anymore, but some at Eight Mile still called them worse. Half of Detroit had burned down in 1967, and then half the white people moved out, and how was he supposed to even half understand it? Did it matter how much you sold for if you were being sold for real? No, the answer was no. So, this guy points a gun at him and leaps—more like stumbles—over the counter to the cash register. Like Hawk, the guy—his age, or close to it—called him "Mother Fucker."

"Open the register, Mother Fucker."

"Earl Mother Fucker to you, Dude," he could have said. He could have gotten shot like Jerry, who wheeled around the corner of the walk-in cooler and shouted, "Drop it!" like he'd seen in the movies, maybe imagining another line for his resume next time he ran for school board.

The kid whirled and shot. Like in the movies. A dumb unlucky shot that dropped Jerry instantly.

"You shot him," his friend said. "You fucking shot him," and they ran out and did not take a dime.

Earl briefly did a terrified dance between Jerry's body and the store's pay phone, before deciding to call the police first.

———————

The slave auction was halted the first year a black student walked in the door of Eight Mile High. No one could imagine a black kid up on the cafeteria's auction block when that had been our country's history. The school's one-quarter black now, with a fair percentage of Middle Eastern immigrants. The Abbos family, Chaldeans—Christians from Iraq— bought Max's and fired everyone so they could hire family, which caused some resentment in the neighborhood, despite being in the great American Dream tradition.

They kept the bulletproof glass, though they replaced the floor and coolers. They expanded the wine choices beyond bottom-shelf fortifieds like Mad Dog and Cactus Jack. Earl and Angie continued to have casual encounters on and off until Angie got pregnant and married a greasy-haired accountant at GM and moved out into the outer-burbia. Hawk? What happened to Hawk? Nobody knows. Not even their old paperboy.

The Hawks used to fly the confederate flag. One day, when Earl was collecting the weekly ninety cents, Daddy Hawk, taking his time to count out the change, looked at him apropos of the accumulated nothing of his life, and perhaps thinking that a kid named Earl who also came from the South would share his beliefs, and said, "If you ever see any coloreds near my property, you call the police, hear me?"

Earl could have said so much more, but no one ever gave him a dime for his thoughts. He would've given Mirabelle a dime just to round himself up to an even dollar.

Everyone in Warren met many more black people in the years to come, whether they wanted to or not. Earl's senior year, Eight Mile High even invited a few students from Pershing High—only two miles away—to cross Eight Mile for a visit. For most Eight Milers, it'd been the first time they'd been in the same room with black kids. The white kids and the black kids sat and stared at each other. Their teachers prompted them with vague subjects, but there was no extra credit for speaking up, so no one did. Earl badly wanted to say, "Hey, we got a slave auction here, what do you have at your school?" He was sure that'd be a discussion starter. For one brief second, his hand was in the air—his trigger hand, and it began to shake, so he lowered it before anyone noticed.

Or, "Hey, did one of you shoot my friend Jerry?" Or "Are any of you named Earl?" The nervous teachers had neglected to have the students introduce themselves to each other, which also would have been a first. Chubbs sat in the back grading papers.

Sliver's stepdad, Paul, had tried to scrub off the misspelled racist graffiti from the side of the auto shop building before they arrived, with little success, the attempt leading to the confrontation that led to Sliver's death months later.

"We need to at least show them we know how to spell," somebody said. The parking lot raged with vague bravado threats.

"Somebody'll just paint it back tomorrow," Earl heard somebody else say. Jerry getting shot just fortified the wine called racism. In the yearbook photo from their visit, nobody's saying cheese for the camera.

––––––

Jerry's parents kept calling to quiz Earl, pretending they were trying to solve the crime when they just wanted to accuse him of cowardice for not saving their son. The police took Jerry's unloaded gun as evidence of something. "I did vote for him," Helen told Earl at the wake. "I'm saving the bullets," she said, "for the next riots."

Earl's father took him home, finally, after hours at the crime scene. Leroy led him through the crowd outside the police barrier and drove him in silence. His father was a man of few words. He kept his head down and brought home his union paycheck and never said a thing to Earl about race, or love or anything that did not have a clear, easy answer. If Earl did not do his chores, he did not get an allowance. Leroy was not going to let his son quit his job at Max's, so he had one thing he could not abandon.

As soon as Leroy pulled up in front of the house, Earl got out and ran off down the street. He wanted to run hard enough to lose his breath. As if he'd been holding it in all those hours. Leroy did not chase after him.

He ended up in front of Angie's. Late, and the lights were out. He knocked gently on her bedroom window, and she snuck into the yard in a short filmy nightgown. They immediately began to kiss—fierce, passionate, reckless. And they had tumbled into the grass of her father's perfect lawn. And the damp grass. And the moon's eye. And the one bullet that took Jerry down. Jerry's surprised shock that the other guy's gun had bullets.

Lying naked in the grass, Angie slid him inside her, and he did not care that they had no protection. When a police car rolled down the street and flashed its lights at them, they grabbed their clothes and fled behind the bushes till it passed—looking for Jerry's killer, Earl realized. He dressed quickly and ran again, Angie whispering urgently for him to come back, but he did not dare turn around. She looked magnificent in moonlight or streetlight—her skin was made to glow in the dark.

———————

Angie had broken up with Hawk. Earl struggled for words yet again as they stood in the dusk of the moonless parking lot as the cheap buzzing floodlight kicked on to break the silence.

"Think they'll catch them?" Angie asked. She turned to look across Eight Mile into the unknown.

"Mirabelle freed the slaves," Earl said.

"You're talking nonsense," Angie said.

"Yes, I am," Earl said.

"Maybe we don't have to be in love," she said, "to make love."

"You gotta have protection," Earl said.

"What if there's no such thing?" Angie said. "I mean in here." She pointed to her heart.

"Bulletproof glass," Earl said, though he felt his own lack of protection.

Angie opened the pack of her mother's Kools, and they each took one. Earl didn't care much for cigarettes, but he liked knocking gently against the bottom of the pack to nudge them into emerging. In the store, they sold bubble-gum cigarettes at the candy counter that blew out powdered sugar with the first puff. They put up the bulletproof glass in front of the candy counter as well, though it only served to frighten the little kids.

"If I bought you in the auction, that's what I would have made you do," she said. He didn't ask what. He smelled the menthol of the unlit cigarette.

"You don't have to have a gun pointed at your head to come visit me," she said.

"And vice versa," Earl said. He cupped his hands around hers as she lit her cigarette with a lighter, then she put the end of hers to his until they heard the tiny hiss of it catching fire.

Chief

Obvious nickname for the boy with the mohawk haircut. When it grew back in after the miracle of his graduation and his famous war whoop across the stage, Brad was still, then and forever after, Chief. He grabbed his diploma, and promptly disappeared into a chemical haze. His acne scars deepened into tribal markings, and his stutter worsened. If we sneered at him a bit when we filled up at the Hi Fi station where he worked off and on, he didn't notice, pumping gas into our new cars that we'd built in the Chrysler factory down the road and would spend the rest of our lives paying for.

He'd bend down to push his nonstop stutter-chatter through the slight window crack as if we'd driven in just to pay him a visit, ask for his wisdom on the world, let him finish the joke he'd started last time. His eyes shrunk into glassy pink slits of stoned-out—not bliss, what was it? If he'd been smarter, he could have at least started dealing like my friend Gene. It didn't take *smart* to work in the factory, but you had to tell time and not get hurt.

How could he get fired from Green-Top Lawn Spray? In the high distant suburbs, all the customers wanted was thick green grass. All he'd had to do was push the mowers and spray the poison.

Living in our neighborhood was poison enough for us. Weeds were welcome with the self-defeating love of our deluded nostalgia.

He drunk-drove the car that killed some freshman kid none of us really knew, running into a ditch on a dark turn on Outer Drive downriver. What were they doing out there, where no one we knew lived? The kid's parents found Jesus and forgave Brad, kept him out of jail, though he never drove again. As far as I know, but my knowledge only extends to the end of the block. It extends to knowing when to start and stop. When to idle and see what comes next. One day, I revved up, and drove away from that square, flat place.

The mohawk gave the Chief a thin opening that allowed him to slip out of the world and above the identical streets we lined with our long, stringy hair where we stood waiting for something to happen. He carried a switchblade at all times but never used it except to flick open and shut, slicing wind. His older brother Cal was MIA in Vietnam. Cal had been a bully, even, or especially, to Brad—maybe his stuttering came from bad ventriloquism.

He doesn't recognize me today, passing him by on Archangel Street on the way to my mother's house on Ashville thirty years later. Even when I beep my horn and stop to idle and wave. He's cutting his parents' lawn, back and forth, back and forth. He's had to live with killing a kid. His cheeks shrunk into bone, and he never married, never left home except to live in the trailer park down the block during his flush years.

Why did he have to go and spray a cat with that poison, and laugh, thinking someone else might laugh too?

Little Stevie Wonder

Stevie Wonder, the twelve-year-old genius, being led off the stage at the Fox Theater in downtown Detroit, and Stevie wants to stay a little longer, and Stevie sings "Goodbye, Goodbye, Goodbye," but he was only beginning. I can hear him even now, the brilliant pacing, "goodbye/goodbye, goodbye/goodbye, goodbye/goodbye/goodbye."

In anticipation of a greater warmth, I pushed myself off the radiator in the cold kitchen of a ramshackle off-campus house—Rita had just walked into the party with Marie. Marie had the fine sculpted definition of a model, but her facial features were so sharp and exaggerated that I wanted to take my glasses off just to blur things up a bit. Instead, I went over to the keg and poured myself yet another beer.

I had the bad habit of being the last one to leave every party I attended. Even the bad ones—especially the bad ones—I signed on for the duration. Sometimes, all you have to hold onto is something that stupid. To be the hardest partier at a small Presbyterian college in the Midwest was a little like being a star Division III football player—fame in a small circle that had no greater resonance, a pebble dropped in the water that left no ripples. I had plenty of time for partying, given that I rarely went to class anymore—whichever was the egg, it came before the chicken. As a recipe for flunking out, the combination was hard to top, and with my spoons and measuring cups, I was following that recipe.

"Marie," Rita said, suddenly in front of me on the wet, muddy kitchen floor. "You remember, from Eight Mile."

Besides me, Rita was the only other person from Eight Mile High to ever attend Alba College, a three-hour drive north of Detroit. Most never made it past Eight Mile and Mound, where the Chrysler plant was taking all comers. I'd paved the drunken path to Alba, and she had followed, blowing clouds of pot out of her smokestack, chugging up the straight, flat train tracks to mid-Michigan.

"I remember," I said. "I was at your wedding." Marie and I were near strangers, despite her going out with Carl Cooper—who'd lived directly behind my house—forever. More than once, I'd seen her and Carl going at it behind his parents' cinder-block garage. In our neighborhood, the cyclone fences between backyards were psychological borders, and I imagine Coop thought no one was looking through the DMZ from our house.

"You were? Really? We never talked. You were in the smart classes, and I was in the dumb ones." Marie was short, so when she blew her cigarette smoke upward as punctuation, it hit me smack in the mouth. I swallowed.

Marie had a killer body. Everything tight and hard, like a doll, but she had this fierce urgency that made her seem taller and both more menacing and more alluring. A doll you didn't mess with.

"I lived behind Coop's house, remember?"

She winced. I thought of the expression "old flame" and wanted to say something clever about lighting a match, but instead just absorbed the wince. Coop was dead.

"I'll let you two old friends sort it out," Rita said. She walked away, and the raucous party engulfed her. Rita and I had a complicated friendship. When she'd told me Marie was coming up for a visit, it felt like Rita might be offering me a shot at her. But if no sparks were forthcoming, and Rita herself was going home alone, it was just as likely we'd end up sleeping together instead. It had happened often enough before. We were allies at Alba, where no one else understood Eight Mile Road, the hard deals we made to get away. The endless cracked concrete, the lack of surface distinctions that made us dig and scrape to find one.

Sometimes all we had to do was exchange a look—across a classroom, the student union, a noisy party like this—and all was well. I knew that she knew what no one else knew. Then—sometimes—we slept together in my tiny room in the Brown House where I lived, along with the other Alba artistes.

She'd taken her roommate, Nina, from Shepherd, Michigan, an even smaller and sadder town than Alba, down to Detroit to have an abortion the previous weekend. That's the kind of thing she knew how to do. She'd run into Marie, and now Marie was here.

"You had a goofy little brother—Victor?"

"Vince. He played football."

She looked me over. "And you didn't."

"No." I took a long swallow of beer. "I worked at The Last Stoppe. You used to come in for cigarettes. Kools."

She raised her bold eyebrows. "Aw, you remember. How sweet." She reached into her purse. "Want one?"

"Nah," I said. "I quit everything."

"Everything?" She paused then, flicking her lighter and bending down with the cigarette between her lips. Her face glowed briefly, then faded back into half-darkness, half-bass-thrum of party-party.

"You have a funny definition of 'everything,'" she said, gesturing toward my beer.

"I would expand that definition further for you," I said.

We stood in silence. Some boy-band covering Stevie Wonder blared from the speakers.

"Beer's not whiskey," I said.

"Little Stevie," she said. "I almost feel like dancing."

Little Stevie. See, that's the kind of thing Rita and I—and Marie—would get. We knew Stevie when he was Little Stevie.

"I was in the medium classes," I said. "I got in one smart class my senior year by accident. . . . I also almost feel like dancing . . . Like this is almost Stevie Wonder . . ."

She wore tight black jeans and a silky red blouse that matched her loud lipstick in a way that immediately identified her as being Not from Here. That year at Alba, it seemed like everyone was wearing blue jean overalls. Farm chic or something. The only thing I liked about them was that sometimes a girl's shirt pulled up underneath, and I'd get a flash of skin from the side.

"What's that mean?" she said. "Almost?"

"Look around," I said, "and tell me."

She stood on her tiptoes and made a show of scanning the room. Her hand rested casually on my shoulder.

"No one here knows how to dance," she said.

I raised my arms in an exaggerated shrug. "This is true," I said. "Can I get you a beer?"

"I'll go with you," she said. "I was in the dumb classes, but I got in a medium class my senior year by accident. It was my only 'A' in four years. Go figure. History."

"That's easy," I said. "Mr. Chubbs had the hots for you."

"I never liked that expression," she said. "'Have the hots for.' It sounds like baby talk."

"Ouch," I said. "Whatever. I thought everybody knew that's how you got an A in History."

"Ouch," she said. "And 'fuck you' to boot."

"I never liked that expression, 'to boot,'" I said. "What's that even mean?"

That got a laugh. For a small woman, Marie had a hell of a laugh. I caught people turning to stare. She lifted a leg and kicked me hard in the ass. "That's what it means." Her boots were high and black and wicked. I put my hands on her hips without thinking and brushed my lips against the hair behind her ear as if whispering a password.

"Watered-down Stevie," Rita said. "But at least it's Stevie."

"Almost makes me want to dance." I laughed.

She poked me with a delicate finger. Rita owned a pair of those bib overalls and had become a little sister of the pothead fraternity. She was making an effort.

"I told you Coop OD'd. Why'd you bring that up?"

"Yeah," I said. "I was just responding."

"There were other choices," she said.

"Like?"

"Like, we shot up together at Rita's once at Christmas a couple years ago?"

"No, we didn't," I said, though I immediately remembered about a half dozen of us on a faded green couch. Her parents had separated, and both of them had temporarily moved out in an arrangement no one even tried to figure out or explain. That left Rita, sixteen, holding down the abandoned fort. She had an older brother, Brad, from her father's first marriage, who lived in the slummiest of the three trailer parks on Eight Mile and sold drugs for a living. He'd stopped by to check on her, and he'd ended up giving us heroin lessons. I was just trying it out. Not like Marie. It wasn't my thing, strangely, though nearly everything else was—particularly, speed.

"You remember," she scolded. "I thought that's where the conversation was going when I left. She brought it up to me this afternoon—'didn't we shoot up with him at your place,' she said."

"She didn't mention it," I said.

"Where is she?" Rita asked. "We don't have to stay. I just thought. . . ."

"I kissed her."

Rita just gave me a brief hard look. "She left that part out."

"And I teased her about getting an 'A' from Chubbs."

"Asshole," she said. "She's proud of that 'A.'"

"I didn't say she shouldn't be. She's fucking gorgeous. I kind of forgot that."

"Have another beer," she said. "I'll go find her."

I led Marie out onto the tiny slab of cracked cement that constituted a patio—large enough for a keg of beer in a washtub full of ice. I turned around to glance at her a couple of times, not sure how that kiss had gone down—she was still there, sliding gracefully between swaying bodies while I played bumper cars off miscellaneous shoulders and hips.

Around the keg stood all guys—T-shirted members of the hippest fraternity of the four on campus, which wasn't saying much. They were playing some kind of quaint drinking game that involved either guzzling their red plastic cups or dumping them on each other's heads.

I looked at Marie and shrugged. She gave me her cup, and I pushed my way through.

"Excuse me, guys," I said with exaggerated good cheer. One of them sprayed me with beer from the tap, which brought roars of laughter.

"Hey, dude," another guy said, clapping me on the shoulder. "He's just a little toasted. No harm intended." He took the tap and filled the cups I still held.

I bit my cheek. I had not been in a fight at Alba. Trying to stay clean and half-sober was using up whatever fight I had left. Skinny, maybe even gaunt, I had relied on my disreputable associates at Eight Mile to keep me from having many parking lot brawls. Somehow, I'd gotten enough of a shady reputation that most guys steered clear of me. Maybe all the drugs gave me a ghoulish hue.

"Whatever," I said. Cold beer dripped down my face. I blinked. Cups in both hands, I could not even make the gesture of wiping it off.

I turned and handed one to Marie.

"I think we should go back in," I said carefully.

"I can't breathe in there," she said under her breath. "Are those friends of yours?"

"If they notice you, we might both be in trouble." I opened the dented screen door and we slipped back inside.

"Is this place turning you into a wimp?"

"I'm trying to be a big picture kind of guy," I said, stepping back in the kitchen, a room I usually staked out for heavy drinking and the lack of expectation for upbeat small talk.

"If that kiss was a mistake, I'm sorry," I said.

"I sort of remember kissing you at a party—at Coop's," she said. "I was coming up the stairs and you were coming down and we looked at each other and. . . ."

"That wasn't me," I said, though it was. That's what I'd told Coop when he grabbed me around the neck later that night, and I was sticking to my story. What saved me was Marie kissing somebody else at that very moment across the room.

"Sometimes I got in the kissing mood," she said. "Coop, all the guys, they went around grabbing other girls, and it was no big deal, but for girls like me and Rita . . ."

"But I just kissed you now," I said. "My doctor says I have no impulse control."

"We have something in common," she said and took my empty hand and pressed it against the crotch of her jeans.

"That didn't just happen," I said.

"Suit yourself," she said.

"What does that mean, 'suit yourself'?"

"I think college messed with your head," she said.

"Everyone seems to agree," I said.

"What kind of doctor talks about impulse control?" she asked.

———————

As Maric and I were making tracks through slushy snow-covered yards, still deciding where exactly we were headed, two Alba police cars—their entire fleet—pulled up in front of the house, parking recklessly at odd angles, then the four cops bustled noisily up to the porch, various metal appendages rattling off their belts.

Marie gave me a puzzled look.

"Aw, they're just here to break up the party," I said. "One of the neighbors probably complained."

"You're kidding. They send two cop cars to break up a drinking party?"

"Well, two is all they have," I said.

"I waited days for them to show up back home after some guys trashed my place, and then the cops only stayed five minutes, mostly checking me out and shrugging."

"Some guys?"

"You know those guys—the guys you owe money to who just have no patience?"

She squeezed my hand. "This Alba place is so quaint."

"I thought it'd be a good place to start over," I said, "but I was followed by the Detroit Demons."

"Isn't that the name of our baseball team?" she said.

"Ha. That's roller derby," I said.

"I'd like to see some of your paintings," she said. "But not tonight," she added quickly.

"I even know the names of two of those cops," I said. "They've stopped me a couple of times for walking alone down the street late at night."

"Suspicious behavior for sure," she said. "Poor EJ, don't you have any friends here?"

"Rita—she counts but she doesn't count."

"I'll tell her you said that."

"I mean she counts double," I said.

As we headed away from the house, we heard the music's abrupt halt into silence.

"Officers Gallagher and Chester—also known as Cheese by the locals. They get lonely out here too," I said. "Like me."

"She's thinking she wouldn't mind sleeping with you," Rita said, "but I don't know."

"What do you mean, *you* don't know?"

"You'd both blame me afterwards," she said finally. "Me, I think I'm going home with Kirk."

"Kirk, the Pappy Yokum in the coveralls with the shitty weed and rich parents?" Everybody seemed to know everybody at Alba.

"Fuck you," she said. "You're always judging everybody. Why'd you even come here? I came to follow you, but why did you come here? Really?"

I set my beer down on the kitchen table. My hand trembled slightly.

"No, you didn't. Don't put that on me. They gave you that sweet scholarship deal." I didn't say *after your dad lost his job*, but that's how it happened.

"I'm not gonna try to convince you—that's not what this is about," she said. She dropped her head, and tears dripped quietly from her face half-hidden behind her long blonde hair.

"I'm here because this place is smaller than Eight Mile and nobody knew me and I thought I could kind of start over . . . You know all this."

"How's that working out for you, three years later?" she asked, lifting her face toward me.

"We got those Scholastic Awards from the Drunken Sailor," I said, "He said this was a great place to make art. Isn't that why we're both here?" The Drunken Sailor was head of Alba's art department and in charge of the statewide Scholastic Arts Contest for high schools.

"'Make great art'? All he wanted to do is get in my pants."

"Those overalls make it easy," I said, and she slapped me. With Marie in town, Rita wasn't wearing the overalls, and in fact was wearing more makeup than usual, putting her Eight Mile face on for her old friend. I was sick of weak beer and the endless AA meetings off campus at the Plaid Door secondhand shop with the townies. She was right about me.

She touched my cheek. "Just a little slap between old friends," she said. A tear streaked her makeup, and she looked so vulnerable that I felt my own tears welling up. I needed her to be as tough as she was. To give me the slaps I'd deserved.

The Drunken Sailor should've been coming to the AA meetings with me. When he'd slept with Rita, it'd stung me a bit, since I'd idolized him. We'd become drinking buddies—a little strange for a wholesome place like Alba, and a funny way of starting over after becoming hooked on anything that had the slightest snag on it in high school.

I suddenly wanted to ask her to come home with me. I noticed Kirk eyeing us warily from across the room—a tall hayseed who looked more like Jethro Bodine than Pappy Yokum. He also looked like he could fuck all night and make you pancakes in the morning.

"Somebody's waiting on you," I said.

"Take care of Marie," she said. "She's out by the curb hugging her knees."

"She seems like kind of a head case—the whole Coop thing . . ."

"She's staying out at the Triangle by Four Corners."

"She's staying in a motel?"

"If that's what you call the Triangle. She said she couldn't stay in a dorm—that it'd be like going back to church."

"Like I said, head case. A smart, sexy head case."

"She gave up God and homework at the same time . . . And she didn't have art like us." I like when she grouped us together into a unit like that, like we were separate from the rest of the world, as if we had a higher calling, even if we were stuck in a lower register.

"Why's she here?"

"Because it's not *there*. Because she seemed almost nostalgic for her own abortion, which seems fucking nuts to me. I was her ugly friend for a lot of years, but she never treated me that way."

I half nodded. My friend Gene was like Marie. Cool in high school—at the cost, it seems now, of the rest of their lives. Gene had lost his license, had done 90 days, was unemployed and living in his father's basement where he cut cocaine on the pool table on which we used to spend hours knocking balls around, determined to be good at something cool, since we were not athletes. Since it was a game two guys could play together without feeling awkward or stupid. His career goal was to move up the drug-dealer ladder, which was always a dangerous proposition because it meant taking somebody out on the rung above you.

"Like me and Gene," I said.

"Except Gene's an asshole, the opposite of what I just described. He always treated you like a chump."

I sighed. "Not always," I said.

She shook her head, resigning from that conversation. "So, cocaine— her drug of choice these days—is out of her price range. So, she's making compromises."

I knew from Gene that she was on the cocaine train—they were some- how still speaking to each other after their ten seconds of marriage—but that train was crowded in those days, so I hadn't thought much of it—but compromise in our vocabulary was a euphemism for something bad.

"She's fucking turning tricks?" I tilted my head in disbelief.

"Making compromises."

———————

Marie wanted to say good-bye to Rita before driving back to Detroit, so we stopped by her dorm. Nina was lying on a couch in the study room.

"He's still in there with her," she hissed. The guy who got her pregnant lived at the jock frat house. He had not been concerned enough to even contribute to the abortion fund. Rita had kicked in some. Even I dropped five bucks in Rita's knit hat in the student union where we all swilled awful coffee as part of being artists. Nina was still feeling shitty, I could tell. I hoped she hadn't spent the night on that couch, but it looked like she had.

I nodded, then looked at Marie, as if to ask, are you sure?

"We're all grown-ups here, right? Hell, I just got divorced. Knocking on my friend's dorm room"—she couldn't say 'dorm room' without a slight sneer—"to get her out of bed is absolutely no problem."

I wanted to ask about that quick marriage and divorce, but she was striding down the hall, her tiny hand already cocked in a fist.

———————

"Hey," Rita said, poking her head around the door half-wrapped in the Indian quilt I was familiar with—familiar with that sleepy smile too.

"Just stopped to say goodbye," Marie said. Rita looked at us for a sign of where we stood, all three of us. I wasn't so crazy about being in the dorm myself on a bright, stuffy Sunday morning—it did feel like church. My two years in dorms—three different buildings, five different roommates—had been disasters. Towels under the doors, ties on door-knobs—we may as well have been running around in diapers, as the frat pledges had to do.

———————

Carl Cooper was black, the rest of us white. *Are* white, while Coop lies in the past tense. A lot of reasons, then, for him to be behind the garage with Marie. We lived in Warren, on the edge of Detroit, right off Eight Mile Road—nearly all white back then, though it was after the riots, so white flight had begun, pickup trucks clumped with sagging beds and scratched linoleum tables, neighbors heading out to outer-burbia, where they imagined they'd be safer. Coop's Mom slipped him over the border when we were starting high school. No new white people moving in, and the ones that remained, like Rita and me, and our families, would've moved if the resources were available.

I mention that because in Detroit, at some point, as white people, we felt the need to mention if someone was not white. Because it says something about Marie that she and Cooper were the first interracial couple I knew, and they stayed together for years. I'm not sure what it says about Coop, or me, that we were never friends, despite our adjoining backyards, despite the fact that my dog got his dog pregnant, and she had puppies they gave away. My dog climbed under the fence—the opposite of what we'd imagined—that's what I want to say.

I drove Marie back to the Triangle and skidded to a stop in the icy ruts of the gravel parking lot outside the door to Room 11.

We sat in my running car—an old Plymouth Satellite with a bench seat in front—next to Marie's Chevy. I think we'd both been in cars like that many times before. In Detroit, every important thing seemed to happen in cars.

"Are you still thinking about me?" I asked.

"What?"

"Sleeping with me?"

She leaned into the far corner of the seat like a cat smart enough not to get surprised or ambushed—small, nimble, fluid. I felt like she could disappear if she wanted to, and that she might want to.

"Why does Rita tell you everything?" she said.

"Why does Rita tell you everything?" I said.

"I guess we have something in common," she said.

"Right now, it's the absence of Rita. In the absence of Rita, let's decide for ourselves."

"Like, take a vote? I think that might be a tie," she said.

"What makes you so sure?" I asked, pushing in the cigarette lighter. I have always taken a comfort in its red glow, particularly at night—at night in the car with my father driving anywhere, always smoking, pushing in that button. When I hear the soft hiss of that coiled heat against tobacco, I know I am safe.

The lighter popped out.

"If you've got 'em, smoke 'em," she said, and pulled a pack out of her small sparkly purse. I offered her the coil, and she lit one up.

"Just give me one drag," I said. Our fingers touched as she held it to my lips and I took a long one.

"Oh, hell, you may as well come in," she said. "That was a shitty party. The night isn't young, but I have to admit it's good to hear your voice, a voice from back home. I don't have to lie to you about anything."

"That's good," I said. "I'm not a fan of lying."

"If I let you into my room in this dive motel, I need to tell you I've got a little case of the jingle-jangles. A big case, actually. I'm too depressed to have sex with anyone . . . Even myself," she said.

"Debbie Downer," I said.

She laughed. "I know Debbie Downer," she said. "You remember, from Coop's parties?"

"Sure," I lied. For a fan of the truth, I was having a bad night. I was only at that one party. Though he had legendary parties—his mom worked nights—which my own parents called the cops on. I was more of a private stoner back then. People, they just got in the way of a lot of my habits.

"We used to sing a song late at night sometimes, 'Every party needs a Cooper, that's why we invited you, Party Cooper.'"

"That doesn't make sense," I said.

"At the end of a party at Coop's, it always seemed to."

"Are you doubling up on being Debbie Downer?" I asked. I got to hear her great laugh again. It was clear you had to earn it, to pierce the hardness, not just scrape against it.

When she turned the key and we went inside, the room was freezing. I found the thermostat and cranked the heat full blast. The blower rattled its old, weary bones while she came into my arms and wrapped herself around me.

"Old EJ," she said. "The legendary EJ."

"Legendary?"

"In Rita's mind."

"I love Rita," I said.

"Not enough," she said.

"She doesn't love me so much anymore," I said. "Not in that way."

"No, not in that way," she sighed. "I married somebody for less than that though . . . She loves you harder and fiercer now that she knows what you are."

I wanted to ask what *what* was.

"Why's she sleeping with that hick?"

"I thought maybe you'd know. We go back to girl fights in the bathrooms at Eight Mile, but since she's been at college . . ." She took her hands from around me and splayed them away from each other as if opening herself up for a needed blessing.

"When I saw her last week, I needed to see her."

"She's a fucking rock," I said.

"A fucking rock," she said. "College hasn't softened her up much."

"Oh, she's a complete marshmallow now," I said. "But I still wouldn't want to face her in a bathroom at Eight Mile."

She slumped into the room's raggedy orange chair, leaving a bed for me. I fell back on it, flinging my arms out, but I didn't bounce. I sunk.

"Come to poppa," I said, reaching up toward her.

"How did you ever become legendary with lines like that?" she asked. "Fucking college."

"Fucking college," I said. "Where exactly are you living right now?"

"Still in the 313," she said, "but close to the 517."

"Why don't you come over here and get closer to the 517?" We were perversely proud of our area codes, even if the 313 meant higher car insurance and various illegal forms of protection.

"You just won't quit," she said.

"Oh, I quit awhile ago," I said. "I just like hearing your voice too. You've got a great pissed-off voice. Rita never told me that."

I thought of nothing more to say, and we gave in to the silence. The room was finally warming up, the radiator calming to a quiet hum so that we could hear nearby traffic from the Four Corners.

"Will you sleep on the floor and talk to me?" she asked.

"Isn't this the plot of an old movie?"

"Yeah, and I like that movie." She turned out the light, but the parking-lot floods illuminated the room with enough light to guide her to my side just as I was rising from the bed to move to the floor.

"Just for awhile, let's do this," she said.

And we did. And because I was not so good at just doing that, she said, "Okay, you'd better sleep on the floor now."

"I never sleep much in hotel rooms after sex. I'm ready to try it the other way." I knelt down next to the bed, and she climbed in under the covers.

"You look like you're going to say your prayers," she said. "Pray for me. Just don't give me any advice. I know what to do. It's the doing it. . . ."

"Yeah," I said. She didn't have to finish. "We both might need some divine intervention," I said. I almost said something about the future, but I didn't.

———————

Rita pulled me close against her face at the edge of the door and whispered in my ear. I loved Rita—I guess I said that already. That's part of the sad part. She would have gone on the lam with me. She was willing to be my desperado partner with a fierce loyalty I did not appreciate enough.

"Can you escort Pappy Yokum down to the men's room in the lobby, then make him go home?"

"Make him go home?" I whispered back, her warm breath tickling my face.

"Kick him in the balls and run—that your style, isn't it?"

"Jesus, Rita," I said aloud. "One time. That was one time."

She shut the door on us. Marie looked over and gave me a curious smile. "You two," she said, "You should really think about getting together."

———————

I should admit now that I slept on the other twin bed in the Triangle Motel, which, although located on a triangular corner, was a rectangular slab of rooms you pulled your car up to, headlights bouncing off room numbers as you drove through ruts, kicking it old style. I guess I was laying it on too thick, sleeping on the floor and everything. Like how I got carried away down at the Plaid Door, embellishing student depravity for the old coots, confirming what they always imagined about those wholesome Presbyterian youths.

———————

In a minute, Kirk came out of the room and gave us a different kind of smile entirely. Rita quickly pulled Marie inside and slammed the door.

"C'mon," I said. "Haven't you ever peed in a girl's dorm before?" I started walking, and he followed.

"No," he said. "Do you really go to school here? I never see you around."

I laughed.

"What's so funny? I've got a girl back home."

"Well, *that's* kind of funny," I said, "but I was laughing about you never seeing me around. How small this place is—never mind. Here we are. *Men*—says so right on the door. Be a man, Kirk."

After he took care of business in the token men's room in the dorm lobby next to the front desk, I put my hand firmly into his chest to stop him from going back up to Rita's.

"Look, Kirk, I went to high school with Rita. Maybe she told you. Marie did too. Marie wants some time with Rita."

He backed away from my hand on his chest, looking at me as if I was speaking some other language, maybe one they didn't teach at Alba. Kirk wore a gray Webber High School Football T-shirt under his bibs.

"We're just old friends," I said.

"Didn't I tell you I got a girl back home?" he said. He tried to push one of his long fingers into my chest, but I backed away, so all he got was air.

"Didn't I tell you I don't give a shit about your girl back home?" I said. I turned and went back up the stairs, passing Nina, who had gone back to sleep. I went into the study room and quietly pulled the blanket over her as she sighed. I shut the door behind me. Anybody who's had an abortion anywhere needs a blanket tucked around them—even I know that.

I could hear music coming from down the hall, and it wasn't Sunday hymns.

I knocked, and the door opened by itself.

Rita was wearing her bib overalls with nothing on underneath.

Marie was wearing the same thing as yesterday and looking just as beautiful, except for Rita's asshole hat, an Alba tam o' shanter that said GO SCOTS on it.

"Nice hat," I shouted above the music. Rita turned down the music a hair.

"We were dancing," she said.

"Rita says you call it her asshole hat," Marie said. "I'm wearing it because I'm an asshole for not sleeping with you last night."

"I thought you did sleep with me last night," I said.

"If you count sleeping in Dick Van Dyke beds."

"Dick Van Dyke on a bender with Mary Tyler Moore wakes up in seedy motel."

"Such a gentleman," Rita said. "He's never done that with me. He just jumps right in the sack."

"I'm beginning to think that's my problem," I said.

"It was enough for me to spend a night in The Triangle," I said, "before I graduated. Well, almost enough."

"What'd you do with Kirk?" Rita asked.

"Are you really going to graduate?" Marie asked.

I thought about telling her the truth, but it wasn't worth spoiling the room's good vibe. "How did things go with Paps last night?" I asked.

Rita and Marie looked at each other.

"I kicked him in the balls and ran," I said, "just like you told me to."

"What if he comes back?" Marie asked.

"If he comes back, *I'll* kick him in the balls," Rita said.

"He was that good, eh?" I said. I turned to Marie. "I'm glad you changed your mind. Got time for a quickie before you hit the road?"

The wrong thing to say. And I'd been on such a roll. Quickie. It was the way we talked in Detroit, but not to someone who'd been making compromises. Marie and Rita looked at each other like they did when I asked about Pappy. I was jumping into something I should be tiptoeing around.

"You like me, don't you?" Marie said softly.

"Yes, I do," I said. "I shouldn't . . ."

"I know," she said. "You shouldn't." She pressed a tiny painted fingernail against my lips.

I was imagining her naked with that plaid tam tilted at a rakish angle even as I apologized.

"You're not an asshole," I said. "I would've taken you to the prom, by the way."

Rita laughed, "Oh, the shit's getting deep in here. Can you picture any of us at a fucking prom?" She'd forgotten I'd gone to mine.

I'd taken Rita to Gene and Marie's wedding because I had no date, and we'd ended up screwing on her parents' living room floor at 3 a.m. Talk about a cursed marriage—Gene and his lovely bride Marie were separated within six months. He never let a wedding get in the way of a good party—coke for everyone! No one seemed to remember that I was there. Rita and I had pretended we were at a prom all night. I hadn't mentioned my prom experience then, and I'm not going to get into it now.

"Can I borrow that hat?" I asked.

Rita reached over to her stereo. "You know what I was thinking about all last night while I was here with Pappy?"

Without waiting for an answer, she cranked up the volume on "Fingertips, Part 2," by Little Stevie Wonder. Part 1 was okay, but nothing like the joy of part two. The purity of it still overwhelms me. That song, and the entire double album, *Songs in the Key of Life*—a mix tape I'd made for Rita.

"I'm copying it for Marie," she said.

We nodded our heads to the beat in unison.

One night, Marie pulled up next to Gene's gold Impala in the high school parking lot, a car full of girls spilling out the windows.

"Is EJ in that car?" Rita had shouted from the back seat.

I crouched low onto the floorboards, wishing Marie was looking for me instead.

"EJ? I haven't seen that asshole," Gene said, and Marie pulled away in—she was driving Cooper's Mustang. Coop—Mr. Cool.

I always liked the build-up of the song, "As"— you end up on this boat with everyone pulling on the oars and you're gliding down a river into the limitless sea, into the sunset. Seven minutes of it.

We began to dance, one song bleeding into the next. Tiny, like every dorm room, and like every dorm room, either bone-chill cold or sauna stuffy—the heating system slow to adjust to what was going on outside in the actual world, so on that sunny Sunday in February, bright dazzle off snow, we began to sweat, and not just a drop or two.

Marie unbuttoned her silky red blouse to reveal an equally silky red bra. Rita undid the clips on her overalls, and they dropped down to her waist, revealing her sweet, sweat-beaded breasts, and I took off my T-shirt with the logo from the only album by Detroit, a local supergroup led by Mitch Ryder, featuring their classic version of Lou Reed's "Rock 'n Roll." The three of us in varying states of undress. I always liked that phrase, "varying states of undress." I use it as often as I can.

Little Stevie was growing up on the 120-minute cassette, and Aretha was waiting on the other side of it. If you can't dance to Stevie Wonder, you may as well be dead. Feel free to take off your clothes—Stevie can't see anything. Though we stopped with our tops. I don't want to get too far ahead and into our rocky pot-holed futures, so I'll stop there too. There wasn't much room to dance in that tiny square cluttered by two beds and two desks, but we knew how to make room.

Cutting

My ex-sister-in-law used to cut my hair in their kitchen behind Bronco Lanes on Ryan off of Eight Mile in the House that Cocaine Built and Destroyed. I just gave away the ending. So much for suspense. So little for reckoning. In the quiet afternoon kitchen of neutral refrigerator hum and temperamental dishwasher thrum she'd clasp my head in her hand and snip snip/and cigarette dangle/and dip to ash. She'd dropped out of beauty school (see *Cocaine* above). Cutting coke on the ping pong table in an otherwise typically desperate moldy Warren basement, all lines blurred. Snip. Puff. Snip. Puff. My brother Vince off in his truck hauling long distance, hooking up in parking lots or cheap motels. Driving was better than jail, though getting high, that was better than anything. Even being married, it turned out. Everything turned in the back of that brown fridge. Who counted on heroin as the next s/tumble? A lot of math on the test, and everyone flunked. She wouldn't take my money or let me sweep up. She loved my brother—enough? I was the young dope who once sold his own car for coke. She'd learned how to start, not finish.

For me, afternoon shift at 3. For her, two babies napping. She rarely smiled, but when she did, loneliness shrunk lowercased beneath the dim beige curtains my mother made to hide what she dimly suspected. Her parents died young. Ours embraced her tight, and squeezed. On the line at Chrysler's, I didn't care much about hair one way or another—just keep it out of my eyes, off my sweaty neck. Why not cocaine? Years of fucked-up frenzy, all of us riding in the white limo we couldn't afford. She had a small mirror to show me the results. That, and a sandwich for the road. In lieu of a bump. Or do I have it reversed, or do I mean, revered? To sit. Still. In the slowed afternoon sun of that kitchen. Hard to stop the momentum of a semi. I didn't see her for twenty years, and then I did today. Baptism for a grandchild. We stood together watching the baby cry. "Who cuts your hair now?" she asked, to have something to say. We listened to hair falling.

Beating Around the Bush

In my mind, I still need a place to go.

—Neil Young

But as it hath be sayde full long agoo,
Some bete the bussh and some the byrdes take.

—Anonymous

Beating around the bush beats diving into the bush and getting scratched up. When you beat around the bush, your reward is seeing birds rise and swell into the sky. The ones that don't get shot.

I took the stairs two at a time, bounding up onto the old wooden porch of what the artist types at Alba College called the Brown House. Legendary abode, and I was moving in, replacing Ned Savage, a sage, bearded

Brown-Houser who had graduated the previous spring. I was a junior of fair-to-middling standing who had bottomed out of the dorms after five roommates in two years, ecstatic to have the magic brown door open to me, the only new artist, joining Mark and Mark, Flo and Angus.

My hair was short, due to parental control three hours south back in Detroit. But I planned to grow it long. I kicked my boots off in the mudroom with the enthusiasm of an Australian rules football player, though we were in mid-Michigan in the mid-70s, playing at languor and not caring. I dropped my ironic Boy Scout backpack and army surplus duffle bag on the floor. Angus looked up from rolling a joint at the scarred wooden table where I would soon be drowning my Cheerios with powdered milk.

"Moving in—already?" he asked. I held out my open arms to him, but he had already bent down to refocus on the matter at hand. September 1. Classes started on the eighth.

———————

The pause before the "already" gave me the hesitation blues. Sometimes when you expect a hug and don't get one, your arms flap down like a puppet that's suddenly had a hand removed. Instantaneous deflation, loss of function. Slump of shame.

Maybe that hasn't happened to you. Maybe your hugs are returned a hundredfold. I suffer from premature hug syndrome—a willingness to hug strangers after sharing just one coffee or beer. I suffer from premature intoxication—or permanent intoxication. I'm like a dentist with a drill, addicted to the sound. Nothing I've just told you adds up to anything positive, even in the latest version of the new math that I unsuccessfully learned in one of my elementary education courses, despite being assured the new math was organic, more like art. How could I teach math? I just wanted to paint with my fingers and cut construction paper into swirly shapes and eat glue and have a magic box of tricks like Captain Kangaroo or Poopdeck Paul, my childhood TV idols.

That fall, I attempted to grow the beard, but I was not sage, so it came in patchy and scratchy. I was sagebrush, and the artists of the female persuasion could not be persuaded to tumble with my tumbling tumbleweed. Until I met Greta, whose skin could handle a few loving, hairy abrasions. Her own hair coiled unruly, springy, fizzy, around her head, for she too was an artist.

To get permission to live off-campus at tiny Alba, still trying to cut off its Presbyterian roots while blossoming into a hip liberal arts enclave—how to blossom without roots, Alba's dilemma—you had to be either the child of a faculty member (and theoretically living at home), or have a medical/ mental health excuse. I got a note from the old doctor my grandmother had worked for—he whipped out his Rx pad and wrote up a script for off-campus living. I couldn't read his writing, and it's probably just as well. Also, my five previous roommates may have tilted the scales in my favor. I was painting an abstract series called "Ex-Roommates." I was all abstract—or, nearly. Sometimes I stuck in a tiny face peeking out from the edge of a canvas painted as if it was peeling back. I was big on inside jokes, the biggest being that I had talent.

Ned Savage was a John Lennon-bespectacled temperamental genius. I was tempted to change his name in this story, but what could be better than Ned Savage?

As a freshman living in a dorm, Ned faced down a group of older guys on his floor who came to initiate him—some emasculating bathroom activity that involved underwear, skin, scissors, bananas, toilets, and the liberal use of shaving cream and magic markers. Ned pulled out his samurai sword and charged forward, slicing through the air, backing the big boys down the hall. They never bothered him again. Ned also refused to take the required PE course, yet forced Alba to give him a diploma because he had gotten into grad school at Cranbrook Academy, one of the most prestigious art schools in the country, which had no PE requirement.

For Ned's Senior Project, the Marks manned two large branches cut from a dead tree from down by the polluted Pine River, a giant roll of butcher paper attached to both branches. The plan was to scroll the paper like a cassette tape from one branch to the next while Ned painted the train as it passed by in front of the Brown House—an event that was on the verge of becoming semi-legendary at Alba, despite its complete failure. I was one of the few witnesses, and in my more paranoid moments—like after not getting a hug—I imagined my Brown House residency as just a way of keeping me silent about the sad details of that event.

I can already tell that my own paper is getting wet, falling apart, the boxcars of the story blurring, rearranging themselves into awkward hulks, derailed, rusting on the sidings. Nothing in this world stays on the tracks. Ned should've known that, shouldn't he? Ned refused to call me EJ, my high school nickname, while I was hanging out at the house auditioning for his spot. The others in the Brown House took his lead, as they seemed to do on everything. Maybe he thought it was immature to use high school nicknames or nicknames of any kind. The Brown House liked going formal, like it was an inside ironic joke. I somehow never got that joke. The name Ned was short for nothing.

Ned's was a big palette to fill, but I couldn't even grow his beard. I was both kind of crazy and kind of an artist—why wasn't that enough? Even when no one wears shoes, sometimes you feel like you're supposed to fill them, or that you want to fill them, to be a capital A Artist. After failing the written PE exam, and the physical exam, I had spent the mornings of my first semester circling the track with the smokers and chubsters, trying to cough out the cold burning ball of shame, dying for a cigarette.

I was crazy, but not in any flamboyant samurai way. The sword had hung above the nonfunctioning Brown House fireplace, and after Savage moved out, taking it with him, nothing had replaced it. The blank wall stood out, haunting the houseful of artists. Where'd Savage get that sword? I was crazy in the imaginary-conversations-and-insomnia-toolbox kind of way.

I played guitar with the two Brown House Marks—maybe *that* helped me land the spot?—and we performed at The Coffeehouse on campus. That was its name: The Coffeehouse. Alba had the imagination of a dot, which was how big it was on the map of Michigan. Not even the size of a mole. More of a speck in the flat middle. One of those specks on a computer screen that you think might be an errant period until you rub it and it disappears.

So, how did we end up at Alba, us Brown House Artistes? Blame it on the Drunken Sailor, the Harold Hill of the Art Department, who, in his lucid moments not drunk or chasing coeds, was a visionary provocateur Svengali huckster. He really wasn't much of a painter and rarely showed his work. A salesman for painting, he somehow got put in charge of the Scholastic Arts High School Competition for Michigan. At the annual awards banquet, he performed a stand-up routine that had misfits like us hypnotized into thinking that in order to be *true* misfits—I mean artists—we must, oh, we must go to this small college in the Middle of the Mitten. I never liked mittens, and how good is only one of them? Or, perhaps the perversity of the one mitten drew us there—or the myth of safety in its soft palm.

The biggest hug I did not get was from Florence. Florence—"don't call me Flo"—the hippie chick who would not stand for being called chick, particularly by me, an uncouth upstart from Detroit who drank large quantities of beer and belonged not in the Brown House but in the frat house down the street, according to Florence. I called her Flo. I possessed a level of pettiness that had helped me run through all those roommates, though I always claimed it had to do with the institutional structure of the dorms and the lack of imagination of said roommates majoring in things like Business or Math or Jesus. Flo and I rubbed each other the wrong way. We never found each other's soft spots. We just banged into each other and sent off antagonistic sparks. I had a Detroit state of mind from working at Chrysler's during the summers—rough around the edge—all edge, no curve. The Drunken Sailor might say that I was getting in touch with my animal self. We had a lot in common, me and the Drunken Sailor. Too much.

Florence was such a hip artist, she had dropped out of school entirely. We'd started out at Alba together as freshmen and had been in an awkward Spanish class together. Only four students in the class, and one, Jésus, was a native Spanish speaker. The fourth was Kirk, a small-town dolt who proudly said in class one day that the only girl he'd ever kissed was his high school girlfriend. He drove home every weekend to see her. Flo and I tried to bond over our dislike for Kirk and the professor, Hilda, a large German woman who spoke Spanish with a German accent and was, as we'd say in Detroit, a ball buster. Nobody messed with her. Thus, a class with four students.

Florence lived in the Brown House with Angus, her mellow dope-smoking, bagpipe-playing husband from Nova Scotia, who had come to Alba on a piping scholarship, for we were the Fightin' Scots of Scotland, USA, as it said on the city limits sign (Scotland, USA, a step above being Edmore, home of the Potato Festival, or Midland, home of the Water

Pollution Festival). Angus had just graduated but was sticking around. He'd married Florence for some obscure reason—rare for young artists to get married back then. They never told me that story, a story that might have made us closer—I believed it involved compromise and defeat, money and family. I believed it involved abandoning principle, something I had a special talent for and would have liked to discuss.

A hug that you do not get is an ugh.

Angus quit playing the pipes and adopted a hash pipe instead. He worked at the Hi Fi filling station over on West Superior next to the Plaid Door second-hand shop. Stoned, he took such great pleasure in washing windshields that he tested the patience of Alba's already-patient inhabitants. They'd tip him to get him to stop, beg him not to check the oil.

Florence's best friend, Greta, was six feet tall, and Flo was five-one or five-two. But they were not Mutt and Jeff chicks—okay, no more "chicks." Detroit seemed light-years behind various national curves, all the progressive ideas swinging wide from Chicago to New York, skipping right over the Motor City, or else the noise from cars and assembly lines and ear-bleed music kept us from hearing them whispering past in the Midwest wind. The Drunken Sailor was from Ohio, where I don't think they sail much. We were marooned on his pontoon boat in the cornfields of mid-Michigan, pretending they were the sea. Or perhaps, as Flo said time and time again, I was just an asshole.

The Drunken Sailor was looking for enlightenment at a small Presbyterian college in the middle of nowhere and instead became a drunken womanizer, flying under the Free Love banner. He led late-night sessions where we'd sit on the floor in a big circle and recite Indian chants over and over. It appeared that he didn't have a large repertoire, or maybe repetition was the point. Many nights, we ended up on the floor of his living room, all of us drunk, while he figured out who he could chant up into his bed later. Chanting seemed like a weak substitute for getting wasted. Or, a cover for bad behavior. We went along with it because it seemed crazy: Go Vinda Jaya Jaya! Block that punt!

Apparently, he had once attended The Conference on the Great Mother where he'd learned the chants and lost wife #2 due to excessive skinny-dipping. That wife, Rachel, still lived in town and taught at the local high school. She called him the Great Mother Fucker.

"He's not fucking *my* mother," I told her at the Plaid Door one night where the local AA chapter met—but that's yet another chapter I swore not to open because it's a long, sad one full of lame excuses.

Rachel opened the first women's shelter in Gratiot County, which had a much greater need for it than most people seemed to realize or acknowledge. I had a crush on her. Bye Rachel!

———————————

"I don't believe all the stuff Florence says about you," Greta said. as we finished our second pitcher down at the Pine Knot, or, as hip artists called it, the Pine K'not. The other students called it the PK, and sometimes I did too.

"Thank God, because most of it's probably true," I said. A brilliant, trippy October day where all the colors—sky and leaves—seemed especially juiced. We ended up at the K'not—okay, no more apostrophe— together because we'd both had grandmothers die in the past month.

She blushed. "No, it's not. I can tell." We missed our grandmothers. Mine, an old Scot herself, Grandma McLeod, had forgotten her place in a book, then forgot to turn off the stove. Hers, a Norse goddess, had been paying Greta's college tuition in defiance of her parents, who did not believe in Art.

I didn't ask how she could tell. In recognition of her certainty, I ordered another pitcher of the watery beer they sold for three bucks a pop. Our legs touched casually under the table in the corner booth where we sat. I was glad hers were long. You may wonder what Greta saw in me. Flo certainly did. Our lanky bodies fit together—that's one thing the Drunken Sailor had right—our animal selves often trumped all reason.

One night in that corner booth, the Drunken Sailor and all of us Brown House boys ceremoniously dumped pitchers of beer onto each other's heads in some bonding rite he assured us was ancient and traditional. After which we were unceremoniously removed from the Pine Knot. The Drunken Sailor, being the responsible adult, got banned from the place for a month and had to drink with the disco kings and queens up at the Alibi in Mount Pleasant.

I think the Drunken Sailor appreciated my capacity for alcohol and my stubborn lack of artistic talent. Coming from Detroit, I had a head start on the rural artists who had only been recently introduced to booze. Eight Mile High, much bigger than Alba College, was surrounded by local party stores happy to sell to the underaged, and a network of older brothers that kept us lubricated long before we had a lick of sense on how to handle the stuff—eventually, the state agreed and raised the drinking age back to 21.

"You, Earl Junior, I like you," he slurred one PK night. "You don't take any shit. Artists take too much shit. Look at all the shit I take to teach here." He gestured around vaguely at the townies slouched at the bar and the empty tables around us. I wanted to ask, what shit, but instead guzzled the rest of my glass and ordered another pitcher—my remedy for everything. "Do you know I'm the same age of Jesus Christ when they crucified him?" he asked.

It might've sounded like I was joking, but Greta and I did miss our grandmothers. They believed we should be able to go wherever our passions took us because they had not been allowed to follow passion in their own lives. They were allowed to be secretaries for convents (hers) or receptionists in doctors' offices (mine).

"My grandmother cut a rose from the bush out back and gave it to my first girlfriend," I said.

"My grandmother brought home office supplies from the convent— paper and pens—and gave them to me to draw with." She folded her bar napkin into a mushy star.

We were weeping in our beers when the Drunken Sailor came in, already under the influence.

"Uh-oh," she murmured.

"Yeah," I said quickly, "Let's get out of here." I knew the dangerous lurch of the Drunken Sailor—his predatory nature, loose, lubricated. His third wife, a former student, had recently left him, and he was on the prowl again, though frankly being married had never kept him off the prowl. The Pine Knot was so tiny we had no way to escape the burly Sailor on our way out, his solid, protruding belly blocking our exit.

"My favorite students," he said. "I missed your striking figure in class last week," he said to Greta, winking at her. Someone mourning her recently dead grandmother was not one to be winked at by her art professor.

"Fuck you," she said. "I was at my grandmother's funeral."

That's just how you talked to the Drunken Sailor in order to penetrate the layers, so he took no offense. Still, I was impressed by her surge of anger.

"Sorry. Let me buy you just one," he said, raising his lecturing finger, but she was pushing past him, emitting a low hum—her most dangerous sound, anger rising.

She shoved the door open, and suddenly we stood in cold, clear, smokeless air, puffing our breath and holding hands because it was getting near mitten time in the mitten (though artists emphatically did not wear mittens), the day's clear skies giving way to starry night chill. I furtively waved to the Drunken Sailor through the PK's lone window, his face distorted against glass, because the sober sailor who channeled his unlimited energy into art was one hell of a teacher. He believed in us, and transmitted that belief through his pores when they weren't busy excreting runoff alcohol and sexist gibberish.

Perhaps you're wondering what happened to the Drunken Sailor. This story's going to wrap it all up in a twisted bow, but then you won't be able to untie the bow. That's my doomed plan.

––––––––––––––

"Mark, Earl, and Mark," the supergroup. I'd wanted to call us "Insomnia Toolbox" but was outvoted by the Mark Alliance. They wanted to be Crosby, Stills, and Nash, without the Young. Toby, the son of an Alba religion professor, wanted to be our Young. He had a cute dog named Nirvana with a red kerchief around its neck that matched his own—the girls loved Nirvana. But Toby could not play the guitar, could only play the Flintstones theme song on his harmonica, and yipped like Dino the Dinosaur and called it singing—even worse than the three of us, who were the vocal equivalent of the poker-playing dogs. Maybe we should have called ourselves the Poker-Playing Dogs. You may wonder about my qualifications, but the truth is that through high school, I'd played electric guitar in a variety of short-lived garage bands—though Alba was all acoustic. Electric vs. acoustic. Another of my lifelong dilemmas that first reared its ugly hollow-bodied head at Alba.

––––––––––––––

Toby's my foil, the character whose sole purpose is to make me look good. He wanted in the worst way to live in the Brown House. The Worst Way meant sitting on our brown porch even when none of us were home. Because his father was a religion professor, he had the off-campus option, and he desperately wanted to move into the role of an Artist—something like me, except he'd never taken an art class before (I did get an honorable mention at the Scholastic Awards—I got so few mentions of any kind, it kind of went to my head). Toby was such a wannabe artist that he made me look like Pablo fucking Picasso. He was a dude of much bullshit and schemes. He wore a beret and had a beret tattooed over his navel, which, in retrospect, was his greatest artistic move, though it looked like a flat tire or a turd scraped off somebody's shoe. He had to tell everyone is was a beret. He'd lift his shirt, then point to the beret on his head to clue you in.

One time, when no one was home, Greta stopped by, looking for me, and Toby, sitting on the porch, followed her into the house (we never locked it). He offered her some of his notoriously shitty drugs and tried to take her into my bedroom. Let me repeat. He tried to drug her, then screw her, in my own bed. All while getting around on crutches due to a Frisbee dog accident, so I couldn't bring myself to kick his ass—in the Alba version of sex, drugs, and rock 'n roll, kicking ass was frowned upon.

Greta and I walked home from the Pine Knot, arms entwined. We stopped at the Brown House, and she spent the night. I'm skipping over the sex, though it was pretty good. Perhaps our grandmothers would've even been proud, but they wouldn't want me going into detail. I apologize to both of them, just in case I open a door in here that they would have preferred remain closed.

My bedroom door opened up into the living room, so any illusion of privacy was negligible. No one wore pajamas. Many true artists apparently did not wear underwear at all. In the morning, Greta had to use our one bathroom off the kitchen, so she stepped out and walked naked past Flo. In response, Flo began having cardiac arrest, or at least cardiac probationary status, at the kitchen table.

"No, no. Tell me it's not true!" Flo shouted, and Flo never shouted. She relied on sarcasm and her middle finger. Greta said nothing. Angus's dog Roof stuck his nose, then the rest of himself, into my room. "Roof," I whispered happily. He wagged his tail like we'd been in on some secret together, and perhaps we were, since he'd greeted me and Greta at the door late the previous night.

I heard the toilet flush and the bathroom door reopen, then a knocking against the table that turned out to be Flo's head banging.

And still, Greta said nothing as she walked back into my room. Roof knew her well—Greta and Flo often walked Roof together down by the Pine River, though it was polluted by a chemical accidentally released when cow feed got mixed up with a fire retardant chemical upriver in Midland—the true "Middle of the Mitten," according to their sign. Roof had to be on his leash so he didn't drink the water. So did I.

Roof licked Greta's kneecap. Flo called to Roof, a frantic edge to her voice, and he slowly sulked out the door, though I could tell he would've liked to hang out with us and swap tall tales. Greta closed the door and unbuttoned my flannel shirt, and thus I skip over the good parts yet again.

I apologize to Greta too—a very private person—though she is dead. Dead less than three months after that October night. I should have told you sooner. My puppet-less arms have been limp and grieving for years. I've given up painting except for the dabs I make for my elementary school art classes, giving them my Goofy the Disney Dog laugh, which never fails to amuse, though I'm not sure they even know who Goofy is. And that's all right. Dogs from the past, even beloved ones like Roof, can be forgotten more easily than any lover. Even from one-night stands where you never learned their names—you still remember that night in Lansing, that campground at Higgins Lake, the bathroom stall at Burger King. No one took the hand out of my puppet body like Greta.

Speaking of Goofy, are you still with me, despite painting Flo as a villain? Don't worry, I'll muddy that up down the line if you stick around. Did I say I was a lousy painter? Clumsy with the brush? That I couldn't draw the human body, naked or otherwise, without turning it into a cartoon animal? Abstract, sloppy, I covered my jeans with paint, then wore those jeans everywhere.

———————

I will lick Greta's kneecap like a happy dog in the afterlife. No one I know owns any of her bright, primitive paintings, and I'm not going to be able to conjure one for you here. During a strained, staticky phone call one drunken midnight, her mother—who I would have met had I gone to the funeral, who must also be long dead—told me they'd gotten rid of them all. I was surprised she knew my name, knew enough to despise and blame me. Maybe we should have named our band Guilt by Association. Maybe I didn't really know Greta—she exuded a lot of bright light, and I think too often I shaded my eyes, looking down or away.

———————

The funeral was held in a Detroit suburb, Plymouth, named for an automobile I once owned. Plymouth Satellite—isn't that a great name for a car? What would Ned Savage do with a car like that? What happened to Ned? Did he become a stoned-out tramp wandering the shores of Lake Michigan carving sand sculptures for tourists, as the Mark Coalition claimed? They added that he wintered in Clearwater, Florida, doing the same thing, and that makes me think, yeah, maybe it's true. But what about the samurai sword? Why isn't he still swinging it at the bastards? The wedding invitation our friends Rita and Jake sent to him landed somewhere in a land of no RSVPs.

No, I did not go to the funeral. I thought it better to return to Alba from Detroit, where I was spending Christmas break getting stoned with high school friends, and share my grief with Florence and Angus and Roof and the Marks. I believed Brown House artists should scoff at burial rituals, the formaldehyde and piped-in elevator music of sadness.

Or maybe I was just copping out.

I'd driven back to Alba at night after getting the news in a terse phone call from Chip Charles, Dean of Student Affairs, who'd given me permission to move off campus the previous spring. Chip—though I called him Chimp—was a decent man who knew what was what on campus and off, and had seen me and Greta doing full-body hugging on the steps of the chapel one night.

Late. I'd been crying for most of the long, straight drive up U.S. 27. Other than my grandmother, no one I was remotely close to had died. Certainly not anyone I'd been in love with. Where was my grandmother when I needed more roses?

The house was dark, but when I turned the lights on, I saw Flo curled up in the stained recliner in the corner, Savage's old throne. She looked up at me with her swollen eyes. I hurried across the room to hug her, but when I bent over, she shoved me away so hard I stumbled backwards. Roof wagged his tail, looking from her to me, me to her. He needed a walk down by the river, but no one was taking him.

" . . . and then the fucker starts getting the paper delivered and expects us to split the cost. What were you thinking, letting him move into *The Brown House*?"

Flo considered it a sacred palace, and that when I'd been scaling the ramparts, they should've poured boiling oil on me. Their voices drifted down the stairs—they hadn't heard me enter, returning from a long night with the Drunken Sailor at the PK. I was sure Angus would defend me—we got stoned together nearly every night.

"Yeah, he's a selfish bastard," Angus said. "Mark said we should tell him to move out in December."

I did not know which Mark, but it did not matter, since they never disagreed. The Marks shared the other upstairs room. They were disciples without their guru since Savage left, and sometimes it seemed like they were taking it out on me for not being Savage. Or even wizened.

I wanted someone to say why they *had* let me move in. Did Greta know? Why did Greta not get to move off campus when she had a note from *her* doctor—a real note from a real psychiatrist? Had I been the backup choice after she got stuck back in the dorm?

"The asshole leaves the kitchen a mess, pisses all over the bathroom floor, eats twice as much as anyone . . ." All guys have bad aim, don't they? It must have crushed her—both when Greta had to stay in the dorm, and when Greta stopped staying in the dorm to sleep with me in the Brown House.

I walked into my room, not loudly or softly. Roof came clacking down the wooden stairs and nudged my crotch as I sat on the bed. I pushed him away. Everything Florence said was true. I had never shared a house with anyone. I didn't get the *share* part. I'd gotten by on my artistic hair and ignorance. I was as bad as Toby and his dog with the kerchief.

Roof, usually a mellow mutt, always snarled at Nirvana. Once he yanked off the red kerchief with his teeth. Nirvana has his own sad ending. Maybe I'll skip that too. My notes from those years are written in a code I can no longer crack. Or maybe they're just gibberish.

I canceled the newspaper and opted out of our food coop where we each kicked in a few bucks a week, but that just made mealtimes completely weird. I ate potpies alone in my room and stopped getting stoned with Angus. The Marks both found girlfriends and stopped eating entirely, as far as I could tell—I suspect their girlfriends snuck them into the cafeteria—the slumming artists from the Brown House, Mark and Mark, rocking the cafeteria without Earl, their best singer.

I think Angus missed the newspaper. Roof did too—one less thing to bark at in the morning. Maybe Angus even missed sharing his after-dinner bowl with me. He took up playing Yahztee after he got stoned. I could hear dice rattling through the wall as I pondered the fact that it was Angus's dope we always smoked, and I had been a total mooch.

The dice drove the Marks crazy, and Flo herself took Roof for more walks after dinner. Angus spiraled into mindless marathons of rolling dice, counting dots. He was a sculptor with no money for materials, but enough for pot. The filling station job was not filling. The bagpipes had disappeared—hocked? He was as lonely as me, I think now, but we never talked about loneliness.

Though Roof was Angus's dog from before they met, Flo had taken over caring for him. The only woman living in a house with four other guys. I never thought about that. What about her loneliness, and having to suddenly share her best friend with me? Me, who she truly despised, and with good reason?

But how did she know I was the only one with bad aim?

A million different shades of white—just go to the paint store. You start to look at them, they all seem the same, but if you stare long enough, you can see the difference between Linen White and Dover White, between Milk Moustache and Going to the Chapel. But when you love somebody and they die suddenly, and you are young, you can throw all those paint chips in the trash. Nothing Subtle—that's your only color.

Rock/paper/scissors. The train's rushing by, and there's no fucking way, Mr. Savage, that you can paint the whole damn thing, and trying just makes you this pretentious artist with a goddamn kerchief around your own neck. The girls don't think it's cute anymore, just another brilliant flameout. Right, Mr. Neil Young, who's seen the needle and the damage done?

What was it with kerchiefs? Back at Eight Mile, I would've gotten mocked—or worse, gotten my ass kicked—for wearing one.

I haven't told you how she died. *How'd she die, Mr. Hug Man? Mr. Crazy Artist? Isn't* that *why you didn't get a hug from Flo?* My job in life has been to beat around the bushes. How am I doing, grandma?

If you're sleeping with someone and you must be apart for a period of time, due to something like a semester break, so you call them up because you miss them, and that person does not return your phone calls—I'm making a deal with you here—since I skipped the sex, I can skip the suicide, right? The artist route. Sometimes the clichés will kill you.

Where's the Drunken Sailor been? Once I was tossing a Frisbee with him and tried to catch it in my mouth like a dog and ended up with an enormous fat lip. It did not become legendary.

In class, the Drunken Sailor was magnificent, stalking the room like an unruly, loveable bear, assessing your work with bad puns and inspirational wizardry, sometimes dismissing a bad painting so thoroughly and compassionately that you knew he was right, and that he'd only done it because he cared. I think we all loved him after a good class, but he scared us—part of us knew, deep inside, that he was part Music Man.

Mark, Earl, and Mark, headliners at The Coffeehouse. *The Alba Almanac* staff photographer took our picture, and the Activities Board stuck it on posters around campus. We looked cool on those posters—like we might even be able to harmonize on deep, sensitive, profound folky folk songs. We sat in The Coffeehouse drinking The Coffee during The Day, staring up at a giant Savage painting of angels with breasts that the school purchased in order to make it up to The Brilliant Artist for their rude treatment of him regarding physical education. On the verge of breaking up before our second gig, we argued over the set list. What would the Activities Board do without our activity?

Maybe I should go back to our first gig, so you can feel the loss of this potential supergroup: as we play, I see, at a table in the back, Flo and Greta and Angus sitting together. From that distance, and through that romantic candlelight on each table, I believe we're all going to be friends. That Greta and I will get married early, like Flo and Angus, to please dead grandmothers or get health insurance or just because we love each other so damn much. Maybe we will all be neighbors or live together on a communal farm. The applause is nearly deafening.

And it carries over so that when Greta and I return home later, Angus is playing Yahtzee at the table with Flo, who says, "You guys just need to rehearse a little more," and I take it as a compliment until she adds, "just not here." But we all laugh.

Angus and Flo didn't have any money, but none of us did. I didn't know what "unforgiveable" meant, or how the world shaved its fine distinctions and let them run down the drain so that when it looked in the mirror all appeared smooth, indisputable. So, in November, when I got Flo fired from her job as a night janitor at the Masonic Home—or she thought I got her fired—the Brown House filled with a deeper, weighted silence and suspicion, and I myself began to doubt what I'd said, how much I'd tilted the scales.

In Alba, like in many small college towns, the friction between town and gown was abrasive and harsh, while the borders were fluid and amorphous. What bars to go in, where to shop, who to look in the eye. The pizza place was neutral territory, for it relied primarily on the campus for its customers. Many students called the locals "Albanians"—not a compliment. As professors' kids, many of our off-campus friends were natives, so we in the Brown House did not use the term.

One late night at Pizza Paul's, I was sitting alone eating a small ham and mushroom when a local came and sat across from me. A cute high school girl, the rebellious, bored type. What she wanted, I'm still not sure.

She gnawed on breadsticks, crumbs accumulating on the thick

geometry textbook she seemed to be using as a prop for her elbow, and for our conversation.

"We're so poor, one of my housemates steals toilet paper from her job for us," I told her at some point.

"Where's she work?" she asked.

And thus, and thus. So when Flo got busted, a thick roll of the good stuff in her backpack as she headed out after her shift, she believed they had been tipped off, and the TP detective who caught her said as much. Not much action for a security guard at an old folks home.

The squealer could have been a co-worker, but Flo did not think so, which left a very limited range of potential suspects. Having extra free time after getting fired, she dwelled on the issue, refusing to play Yahtzee despite Angus's entreaties. Shake, rattle, roll. She even hid the dice.

"Why would Earl rat you out? That means he gets no more free toilet paper," Angus said. I know it seems pretty coincidental, overhearing things like that, but the Brown House was so small, so old, you could overhear just about everything through its theoretical walls. I'm sure they could hear Greta and me having sex while they sat at the table outside my room. And maybe that too was unforgiveable—my amplified moaning with her only friend. I did a painting called Theoretical Walls, one the Drunken Sailor dismissed entirely. He said theoretical walls were destroying our country.

Loose lips drink sips? Loose lips get slipped? I don't know. Did I rat her out accidentally? Weeks later, I saw the breadstick gnawer passing on the street. When I said hi, she looked right through me, but she was with a local boy, and that mattered on the townie/college continuum.

In Pizza Paul's that night. She'd *liked* the idea of stealing toilet paper from your job. Maybe she shared that great idea, and the information got shared down the line. Or maybe Flo was just careless herself. But after she lost that job, a cold dirge settled over any small interaction between us—like hands stuck on organ keys, throbbing tension.

––––––––––

The Drunken Sailor drove down to Greta's funeral in his brown corduroy sport coat and fat, knotted tie and gave a eulogy that no one remembers. The grief was so thick you couldn't breathe. It was a sauna of grief. Or so I hear.

––––––––––

She dove into the burning bush.

––––––––––

I've been married twice myself, and may be in danger of passing up the Drunken Sailor someday, though I have no idea what his current score is. Today, he would have been fired and sent back to Ohio without hesitation or ceremony after just one of the many incidents involving alcohol, driving, women, and transcendental meditation.

Perhaps I became an art major in college because it was the furthest path away from working in the car plants back in Detroit. In that way, in my charitable moments to myself, I think I was no fraud at all. I picked a path, and the choice of that path itself was an artistic statement. Right, Drunken Sailor?

I have a piece of chalk in my hands, and I am going to draw something on the board that I will erase, or someone will erase—it doesn't matter who. I've been okay with that for a long time. In fact, I've come to love the dusty smell of disappearance.

––––––––––

I witnessed the train painting in fall of my sophomore year, invited to the event by the Drunken Sailor, who was trying, I think, to get me more connected to the Brown House community, hoping something creative might rub off on my paint-stained jeans. He'd taken me under one of his drunken wings, knowing I had come to Alba because of him.

We stood on the gravel driveway to the Blue House so as not to interfere with Savage's view. The Drunken Sailor's long white hair whipped erratically around his unshaven face, and the strong wind whisked our voices down the tracks until the train arrived and destroyed all subtle sound, all human sound, and, on cue, the Marks twirled their scrolls, and Savage—it's one of those pure fall days in mid-Michigan that makes you shake and bristle with animal life—like that day the following year when Greta and I flew into each other in our amateur mourning—dangerous weather—leaves surrendering to that wind, which blew them into flashes of sideways color—and Savage is a mad man with his fat brushes and buckets of paint yelling *crank*, and *faster, damn it, faster*, his glasses jerked off his head by the effort, and then *boom*—train gone, whistle fading down the tracks into silent disappearance. Savage collapses on the ground, or perhaps trips over his own excitement. The Marks stand holding their poles like pieces of bread that have lost whatever might have made them a sandwich. We hurry across the street. The Drunken Sailor terse, sober, teeth clenched around an imaginary professorial pipe. We all realize in an instant, looking at the sheets, that the paint's smeared on the back of them as they rolled. That any idiot could have predicted what would happen.

"Part of the process," Sailor shouts, taking control. "Unroll it all and let it dry," he says to the Marks. They do as they are told, but the wet paint has torn the paper, and despite their slow, careful work, it falls apart so that you can't even tell the front from the back.

———————

Is it true that "fuck you" is the only thing Greta says in the story? I'm leaving her mostly out of this—gone, gone. I was young and stupid, but somehow lived through it. God Save the Queen—ain't no saving the queen—she's going to die just like the rest of us.

Flo's the one I'm trying to win over, now and forever. I'd like to believe she's out somewhere walking that loveable dog and thinking about forgiveness, but that's where the paint smears, the paper falls apart, and all we're left with is one of those song endings when we're not looking at each other so we each sing the final note in a cacophonous mess, as if we're shouting over each other in some argument no one's going to win.

———————

The Artistes painted The Brown House every few years, and that fall, after I moved in, it needed another coat. Rex Hazzard, the owner, lived next door in the Blue House. A gay attorney, a patron of the arts and good bourbon, he owned a number of Savage originals, but the only work of mine he owned was the brown paint I slapped on the outside of that house. Back then, he was stuck in the closet door of that small town, snagged by the need to make a living. Any work we did on the house, he'd take off the rent. He represented the Drunken Sailor in various legal matters.

———————

Here's the part of the movie where I do a montage of what our characters are doing now, after those hazy, daze-y college years: I just introduced Rex, and now I kill him off. AIDS would be the movie choice, given the era, but lightning, which came on just as suddenly, ended his life. Living out his retirement with an ex-priest near Lake Michigan, he was standing on a dock when one of those brutal Great Lakes storms blew in, and it got him. Why'd I introduce him anyway? Because he tried to get Flo's job back, and after Greta died, he came to the house and sat in silent witness, and because I can't remember the name of either of his cats.

Mark and Mark both married women named Kim and look at all their cute children splashing in the backyard pool they share. They're next-door neighbors!

Toby currently makes his living as a weekend mime in Harvard

Square. During the week, he sells drugs in high school parking lots. Maybe he never recovered from not being picked to be our Neil Young, our lost Beatle. He specializes in doing that routine where the walls are closing in.

Let me tell you one more thing about Toby because I'm realizing here—yes, finally—that I come off as a self-centered jerk. C'mon, Toby, you're my foil! When he graduated, he couldn't, or didn't want to be, burdened with Nirvana. He drove him out into the country, opened the door of his pickup—another one of his image accessories—let Nirvana out, then sped off.

If only we could drive out in the country and shove all our inconvenient problems out the door and drive off, assuming someone will come by to clean up the mess. I hear my tires spinning in the gravel just thinking about it.

Savage is discovered by a South Beach gallery owner in Miami and given a free studio apartment to begin painting again. No—no—he becomes an internationally famous tattoo artist and has this job on South Beach where every body is a canvas. He has many sports stars as clients. Everyone loves his pet parrot, Ralph.

The Drunken Sailor's story—perhaps you're not exactly holding your breath on this one. He had an attention span as finite as a tiny tube of acrylic paint—he went from raising sheep to growing pot to writing an obscene joke book that's probably still in print, to writing an equally popular tract on the benefits of meditation. Eventually, he "quit" teaching and became a stockbroker, using his charisma and flair to hoodwink investors and make vast sums of money. He lived happily ever after raising drunken bees and selling honey as a hobby, leaving in his wake all the coeds he'd lumbered into over the years, including beautiful Greta, getting himself banned from Brown House parties and eventually getting nudged out of town by Chip Charles after he became Alba's provost. I learned later that there's a town in Ohio named after his grandfather, and that his father made a fortune manufacturing a substance the military had a hankering for, napalm. Maybe he didn't live happily ever after, but that's another story that would take us to Guatemala, so—

Okay, okay. All the birds have been shot except one, the one Roof would carry gently in his mouth if he were still around, but since he was a dog, I can't pretend he is.

Angus and Flo split up a couple of years later. Quitting college, it turned out, was not such a great career move, even for artists, and if you're not going to have a career, you at least need a job.

Mark1 said they fought about money. Mark2 said they fought about Angus's dope smoking.

When I found out Flo was a lesbian, I heard that clunk of her head against the table again. But did I deserve a *Fucker* just for ordering the *Free Press*, a ten-week trial subscription at half price?

———————————

No, wait—maybe there's a sentimental Brown House reunion at the end. Everyone reconciled, their arms around spouses, and each other—one of those magic train-painting fall afternoons, everybody having a good laugh remembering that fiasco, and the Drunken Sailor, sober and reflective, a veritable Santa Claus of a man, lets the children drag him to the ground as he deflects their giggles and blows. Frisbees and cold beer and grilled meat—and veggies for the vegetarians!

And there's Florence and her lover, who's so good-looking that I'm a little jealous. Flo comes up to me and—I never told you that she had this beautiful smile. She smiled so infrequently—this shy smile, like she's embarrassed for her own happiness, like she's smiling against her own best intentions, a smile that escapes, fresh and new into the world. She gives me one of those.

And if we're really going to bring this full circle, in the tradition of Shakespeare and Oliver Stone and Bozo the Clown, then I should get a hug here, the one I've been waiting for all those years. That healing hug that will allow me to move forward in my life, make my peace with both Greta's—and Florence's—suicides. It's piling on even to write that. Two young lives, and me with a chalk eraser and no samurai sword.

Nah. I ain't getting the hug. I get the smile, and a punch in the gut. My defenses are down, my puppet arms at bay. A soft, friendly punch, but I overreact, bending over and grunting, going down for the count at last. Anything for a laugh, a Goofy laugh.

———————————

Here's the voice-over part where I tell the truth. Maybe the film's showing a stunning fall landscape with colors so rich it looks like the world's on fire. Or maybe it's spring, a lush green wave in a light breeze behind the train tracks. And some birds tweeting, then silence, for I have something serious to say:

The last time I saw Greta, we had a bad fight about my drinking and drug use, and she broke it off with me. Then, she called, and I would not answer. She'd put a pinhole in an egg, then tightly rolled up a tiny message for me and inserted it into that hole. I'll never know what the message said—her mother said there was no egg, but I'd seen it myself. Greta said she'd let me crack it when she thought I was ready.

I wanted to avoid the tortured-artist suicide cliché, the one so many films are built around. Did I tell you I'm a film buff now? Moving pictures, real trains in motion, going past in the dark theater. I've come to be a spectator to the world. I know that's not such a great idea, but I faithfully follow the script, despite the rotten tomatoes of ex-wives and ex-band mates. Get a life, they all say.

Her doctor told the truth in his letter to the college—she let me in on that secret, showing me a copy of it, creased sharp, in her thin hemp wallet that smelled of incense. We can watch a hundred people get shot in a war movie or a cowboy movie or a cop movie, but how often do we see someone hang themselves, and for how long do we watch them dangle? Not long, not long. The movie convention shows the chair kicked away, feet hovering, so that's what I'm showing you now. Her long, bare, beautiful, dirty, graceful feet,

I'm leaving the comma there.

Don't ever laugh when someone threatens to kill themselves. You might think they're never going to do something that stupid, that they're just being melodramatic. I know I'm being melodramatic for putting it this way. I didn't want to tell you, but *some* of this has to be true.

I beat around the bush so long that all the grass died, and the dirt turned to mud or quicksand. Maybe I forgot about the bush entirely and was just chasing my own tail. Maybe there were never any birds. Maybe the train slowed down and allowed itself to be captured by the artist known as Savage.

But trains don't slow down for artists, do they? Though once I saw, in a town far from Alba—Pittsburgh, where I teach at the arts magnet school and enter my students' work in Scholastic Arts Competitions—a train chugging slowly over a trestle above the Monongahela River, blowing its whistle loud and constant. I looked up and saw a deer on the tracks wandering across the narrow trestle, ignoring the piercing whistle, the train's hiss and squeal of brakes. Maybe it takes that kind of innocence to slow down a train, and though we were young and naïve, we did not have that kind of innocence.

Okay, roll the final credits. While they're scrolling down, I've got a little flashback for you before the screen goes dark, before you rise from your seat with a shrug and head for the exit:

The train tracks cut right through downtown Alba, then curled around the Brown House (somebody tried calling it the Chocolate House, but *that* never caught on. . . .), then passed the college, so we used to walk the tracks to school in the dewy, serene quiet of early morning. Here's me, Mark, Mark, Florence (taking Roof for his morning walk), Angus (going to campus to score coffee or dope), and Greta (having spent the night, she's heading back to her dorm to shower and change). All of us have our arms out, all of us perfectly balanced, no train, no train, no train in sight.

Dirty Laundry

We only did laundry stoned—one of many things we only did stoned. Clean warm clothes against our faces. Fabric-softener scent. I was cheating on Earl, but we'd signed the lease together. My friend was married. Earl and I never married. We had a lease. Our clothes were fucking, but we were not. Hilarious—or at least not completely tragic—when you got down to it. Stoned, we got down to it. Split it down the middle. Flipped for the last quarter. Three more months on the leash. Lease. He wasn't leaving wife and kids. And kids! We argued. Stung. I didn't want all of it—we had to share the sting. I moved into the cold room where we stored duplicates when we moved in together. Thus, a bed, and the sheets I was washing. Suds sloshed against round windows. Look at those suds, Earl said. I smiled. We didn't talk about whose detergent made those suds. We swayed in unison to the sounds that were not in unison. We loved each other stoned on laundry day. The old women in the Laundromat were grumpy and grabby. Crumply and crabby. They lived in dingy apartments across the street above the Powder Puff. They shouldn't have to go to a Laundromat. There should be a rule: women over 70, someone else does your wash. No questions asked about granny underwear. We were under 30. I pretended to be lying about my age, but I really was 29. He was a kid, 25. That's why you're jealous, I said, you're a kid. I'm not jealous anymore, he said. Just uncomfortable. We need each other for rent, we agreed again. We bent, close, embracing clothes still warm from fucking themselves clean. I could feel his breath. He smiled, his face pink for a million reasons. Stoned, we lived together three more months. Our math was shoddy. The final bills, all in his name. The married man was true to his word, but loaned me money I had no plan to repay, given my unveiled threat at exposure. You do what you gotta to pay the rent, I said.

This is all many washings and dryings down the line. That night in the bright lights of the 24/7 Laundromat on Eight Mile. Outside, no stars, no moon. Windows full of darkness, pressing in, rattling glass. We were like two siblings spending the night at grandma's, smelling her sweet sheets, staying up past our bedtime, telling secrets. In our memories, we were never closer. If you don't believe us, ask the old women who always told the truth. They had nothing to lose. *Ah*, he said. *Ah*, I said. Then I touched his face.

Theme for an Imaginary Wedding

1. After-Party: Making an Honest Man

Tied the knot. Got hitched. Earl knew there had to be other slang terms for what Jake and Rita had just done, but he could think of no others. He loosened his tie, then tossed it at the overgrown rosebush in Rita's parents' yard. It snagged up high in the thorns, knocking down a flurry of aromatic pink petals. He wouldn't be wearing that tie or any tie again any time soon.

Earl had nothing going on. Unlike the others, he'd finished the year twelve units shy of graduation, so he was back doing another stint on the line at nearby Chrysler Assembly. It seemed his only option—live at home, save money, try to figure out what was next.

Jake and Rita's wedding was a first for the Alba College crew—his friends who had either lived or congregated in the Brown House off campus to think artistic thoughts and imagine higher callings, to get stoned and imagine higher highs. Except for Earl, they'd all just graduated with their English majors or Art majors, and, in one case of rare ambition, a double major in English and Art.

Other couples had lived together, were living together, or were contemplating living together now—that, or splitting up due to the imposed reality check of graduation—but no one had actually had a wedding. *Tied the knot. Got hitched.*

Shotgun wedding. Earl remembered that one, but it had the word "wedding" in it and referred to a particular kind of pressured marriage that seemed so archaic that it would soon disappear. The only thing he'd ever shotgunned was a beer, a high school maneuver useful only to show off, get drunk quicker. *Hammered. Sloshed.* He could go on forever with that one. *Wasted.*

Truth was, Jake and Rita did get married because she was pregnant, though her parents owned no shotgun and her mother had tried to talk Rita into having an abortion, which had recently become legal. Her parents, hardly churchgoers, had no moral objections. Her mother was still waitressing in a cocktail lounge part-time. Her father took thirty-and-out from Chrysler and played Elvis on the accordion in a bad oldies cover band called 30 and Out. They'd performed at the Polish Century Club reception they had all followed their xeroxed maps to. Jake's parents were lapsed atheists who now attended a Unitarian Church for the sense of community. Community—Earl was already missing it in a wave of premature nostalgia brought on by the uncompromising lack of freedom offered by factory work.

Earl liked Shakespeare—at the end, either the stage was strewn with corpses or everybody was getting married. Neat and tidy. He thought he should care a bit more that the baby might be his, but since no one else knew or seemed to imagine it possible, he was grateful to play along.

Rita made the announcement in the Brown House living room months before graduation, Jake beside her, shyly abashed. *How?* Earl mouthed to her, suspecting from her stricken face who the father might be. She gave him the slash-across-the-neck sign.

They'd lived in the Brown House together—varying combinations of friends, lovers, and dogs. One night, Jake was in Mount Pleasant for a job interview—an Indian casino opening there, his dream job to deal blackjack—and spending the night with some of his bluegrass friends. One of Jake's odd skills was clogging. Drugs would be taken. Music would be played, clogs would be clogged—while back in Alba, Rita and Earl were playing chess when things got out of hand.

───────────

The wedding was held in Rita's parents' large backyard that ended in weeds at the edge of the slummy trailer park behind their tiny house on Archangel Street, the reception at the PCC a couple of miles away on Eight Mile, then the after-party back in the yard. The Marks had constructed an abstract wooden sculpture and painted it white to serve as the altar. Everyone immediately called it the Rocket Ship. None of those in the wedding party had any money, so the Brown Housers just wore their best dress-up clothes and didn't worry about matching. Since nobody had to buy an ugly dress or rent an expensive tux, Rita had six bridesmaids and Jake six groomsmen. The More the Merrier. Was that a Shakespearian expression?

He had gone to Goodwill, opting out of his plaid sport coat from an ill-advised trip to the Sadie Hawkins dance in high school and going with an oversized yellow one with super-wide lapels. He got a shirt with one of those frilly things you buttoned on, white with black trim. It had to have a name, that thing. It wasn't cummerbund, he knew. His tie had mostly covered it up. Maybe he'd been smoking too much dope—it had quickly become part of his daily routine before going in for his afternoon shift at the plant.

He looked like an idiot, though he imagined himself as a lonely semi-tragic figure, a moody, atmospheric mystery man. How do you dress for the wedding of your true love who is having your baby? Maybe he should have asked somebody.

Cue the bagpipes: Here comes the bride. The Alba *Scots*, and Angus had been one of their stoned-out pipers. Piping at weddings and funerals was the first part of his post-college plan. Angus, decked out in his kilt, showing off his legs to the ladies. Everybody seemed to be goofing on the wedding, treating it as performance art, except for Rita, who had altered her grandmother's wedding dress and looked solemn and beautiful in an old-fashioned kind of way, baby bump notwithstanding. Jake? Jake was going along for the ride, which was what Jake did best.

———————

Rita's hair whipped across her face in the late-night wind. She brushed it away, but it blew back over her eyes in a sexy slant. Earl ached to kiss her. Glowing in the white dress under a dim floodlight rigged up for the occasion, she puckered her lips and blew out a breath to try to lift her hair away. She turned to Earl, and he turned away.

"That dress builds a cathedral around you," he said. He'd half-meant to say something cruel.

"I like how you made the old rose bush formal," she said. "I've always loved their smell. Those roses fall apart so fast, but they smell so sweet."

"I know," Earl said. "I've been here before." He picked up some petals to toss at her, but the wind carried them back into his face.

"So, who am I supposed to marry?" he asked. "Did you pair me with Marie on purpose? Even we both know we're hopeless together. We just don't have the energy to pound the nails in."

"Don't. Don't. You're not marrying anybody anytime soon. Me, I just got tired of all the fucking around. Prematurely tired. I think I started too early."

"Is calling a sex timeout a good reason for getting married?"

"You know Jake's a good guy. He'll be a good father."

"Good. Is that enough? You haven't—"

"When have I ever? I need a smaller frame—canvas—to work on. Just out of school, and everything's already stretching, ripping."

She shivered in the sleeveless dress. He took off the yellow sport coat and draped it over her shoulders. She pulled the big lapels tight around her. Earl shivered.

"Remember when we road-tripped out to Higgins Lake and ended up playing stoned air hockey in that funky go-kart place?" he asked.

"Yeah?"

Earl hesitated. "Forget about it. I lost my tenor. I just have my vehicle spinning donuts in the parking lot."

"I'm glad we were in English classes together. I'll miss that." Rita shed a silent tear. Earl leaned his forehead into hers. He put a gentle hand on the sweet curve of her bump.

"Immaculate conception," he said.

"Hey, what are you two doing over there?" Jake said, emerging from the shadow of doubt.

"I'm blessing your child," Earl said. "Didn't you read your script for the evening?"

Jake laughed. Everybody liked Jake. He'd gotten the dealer job and was in training—the casino opened next month. "Nah, guess I missed that part."

"Gotta read the small print," Earl said. He didn't want to know what Jake knew or didn't know. Rita had been his friend since grade school at Saint Michael's, a short walk down Eight Mile from where they stood, and everyone at Alba cut them slack, shrugging off their genuine intimacy amidst the constant irony that hung in the air like paint fumes, both reassuring and toxic.

Enough slack to hang themselves with. Nobody noticed they were both choking.

"Just remember," Jake said, "the house always wins."

"He's been saying that a lot these days," Rita said.

"All part of the training, I imagine," Earl said.

"Weddings are damn hard to write about if you're being realistic," their English prof, Doc "Pop" Popelewski told Earl as they stood watching the festivities in the yard: three grandmas clapping off the beat, a cluster of deliriously sleep-deprived children staining their good clothes with grass and dirt, old men playing cards under a string of Christmas lights, the stoners clumped in the distance. "That's why Shakespeare ended with them. Real weddings are messy. Real weddings are just the beginning."

Doc had driven down from Alba to officiate. Earl didn't ask how Doc would know since he'd never been a passenger in a rocket ship, just the man doing the countdown. He was ready to call it a night.

The younger Eight Milers and the Alba crowd were the last ones left rocking the yard, lighting up joints like fireflies as the old folks said their goodbyes.

"You might get some material down at the Suez tonight," Earl said. Doc was spending the night at the infamous Suez Motel around the corner. He claimed to be a poet, though no one had ever read a word he'd written. The Suez was reported to rent rooms by the hour.

"Free continental breakfast," Doc said.

"What continent is that? Shakespeare would be writing sitcoms if he were around today," Earl said.

"Would this be a sitcom or a soap opera?" Doc asked, raising one of his thick, unruly eyebrows. Earl wondered if he suspected anything. Doc's life was a broken watch. He was holding it to his ear and shaking it.

"Past my bedtime," Doc said.

"Doc, it's always past your bedtime," Earl said.

The old, bald professor wagged his finger at Earl and disappeared outside the halo of strung lights. "See you at homecoming," Doc said with a limp handshake.

"Right," Earl said. "In your dreams."

"In my nightmares," Doc said.

Chess night wasn't the first time Earl and Rita had slept together. High school and then early Alba had produced a few drunken nights where they'd flipped the sex switch. It didn't take much to loosen up what kept them apart—some level of brain malfunction, and there they were, sliding into and past the slippery spot. That's what was strange about chess night—they were not drunk or stoned.

"So, I see this wedding as a momentous event in *my own* life story," Earl said, echoing something he'd read about point of view. "My first non-family wedding. I'm old enough so I don't have to sneak drinks from half-empty glasses on the tables."

"I guess congratulations are in order then, buddy," Jake said. He extended his hand, and Earl pulled him into a hug.

"Thanks for being here with me on this special night," Earl said. "You're a true friend."

"Fuck you," Jake said, laughing.

"That's the nicest *fuck you* I've ever gotten," Earl said. He turned to Rita. "You're such a lucky bride." He wondered if the baby would look like him, and if it did, who would get thrown out with the bath water?

Rita stood silent, still clutching Earl's sport coat tight around her, her lips pale, on the verge of blue.

"My jacket's too flimsy. Give her yours," Earl said.

Jake obeyed, tossing Earl's back to him. "Here, you can burn this now."

"That's not in the script," Earl said. "But I'll do what I can."

2. Ghost Dance

At the reception, Earl danced with Jake on his shoulders. The kind of thing Alba fraternity boys did at the all-campus bacchanals down at the K of C Hall out by Four Corners, the intersection of M-46 and M-27, where Michigan's Mitten split into four quadrants.

You paid your money and drank your beer, and frat boys and hippie chicks, hippie guys and sorority sisters, all gathered together to get sloppy drunk or just plain sloppy. A neutral site, a DMZ with the implicit whiff of sex in the air burning like a joint or cheap cigar, depending. Nobody fought—room on that dance floor for everybody to "gator" or "swim" or "shake and bake" or just stand along the wall and get stupidly hammered, then stumble down West Superior a mile or so back to the only other stoplight in Alba, where campus began, as they all slowly morphed back into quiet distrust and resentment of the other college tribes.

Earl's was urban semi-hippie artistic-political—a small, motley crew. Most of them had lived together in the Brown House on the townie side of the tracks. Now, they were reunited in the Polish Century Club on Eight Mile Road two months after graduation. They would never all be together in the same room again.

Shakespeare had it right, their old English professor, Doc Popelewski, used to say. End with a stage full of weddings or dead bodies. They called him Pop. He sat nursing a highball in the corner with a couple other favorite professors. "Sex and Death, that's really the title of every course I teach," he liked to tell them. The Drunken Sailor, their art department guru, had not been invited due to fallout from his overemphasizing the sex part at a graduation party.

In his head, Earl was dancing back at the K of C, though here at the Polish Century Club, Jake knocked his knees into Earl's ears with awkward, nearly vengeful nostalgia, trying to stay aboard. The DJ had a thin moustache and the bored disdain of a puppet master. Earl staggered toward him, and the DJ flinched. Jake boxed his ears again. Earl wanted to drop the burden of being the life of the party. It suddenly seemed like such a stupid thing to take pride in.

One flushed night at the K of C, dizzy with lust, he and Rita, Jake's bride, danced out the dented metal doors and into the spring night, staggering between kisses into an empty field out back until they found a place to lie down. What they wanted to do required solid earth to press against—a soft, grassy patch, slightly damp from the day's spring rain or late night's early morning dew. They shrugged off their jeans, then clung together with the repressed fury of years of pretending to be just friends. Afterward, they spent long silent minutes in each other's arms—longer than the sex itself—listening to the first insects of the new year share their secret.

What had happened for the night to allow it, the moon to allow it, for the night clouds to pass over without comment? It seemed pure, without guilt, despite their semi-attachments with others. Suddenly with exaggerated frenzy, they yanked their jeans back on, laughing madly.

Earl dropped him down onto one of the round white tables, and Jake sprawled across it, kicking over drinks and laughing hysterically, trying to catch his breath. Someone's distant relatives stood and backed away from the table with pained, bemused smiles. Where was the bride? Earl would have never given away the bride. He wanted to tell somebody that, but he just drifted away from the table as the DJ shifted into something slow, too slow. It looked as if a group of doctors was surrounding the table, planning an operation to get Jake to stop laughing.

Rita ran back to the K of C. The music inside seemed to breathe and heave with the door opening and closing. The air smelled metallic and human, merging in the bass thrum that scraped their hearts.

They'd never spoke of it, of any of the times they crossed over, then back. To speak of it would mean to assign blame. Blame had no footing on that slick, wet night.

At the reception, no one called him EJ—not even Rita. The world of nicknames was evaporating right before Earl's eyes—at banks, graduate schools, investment firms, ad agencies, yoga studios. Middle initials would resurface on credit cards and ID badges.

Madness ran through the crowd of throbbing tribal motion. Earl watched from the door as Rita ran straight into the center of the dancing circle and disappeared, then he turned and walked away, following slick railroad tracks back to the Brown House, his arms at his sides, his wings folded in.

3. Room Service

Most of Earl's friends were staying at the Suez Motel, a dingy rent-by-the-hour dump on Eight Mile. Young and brilliant, ironic and poor, lighting up a dull weekend on the sleepy edge of the rest of their lives, recent grads of Alba College were doing an encore a month later to celebrate the first of what would be many marriages and eventually a fair number of divorces with nothing fair about them.

Earl had spent the night before the wedding in a room with the groom, Jake. Now it was Earl's room. Despite living nearby, he'd taken the free room to escape his parents' basement. He'd volunteered it for the after-party and was now too drunk to drive home to escape it. Jake and Rita, Earl's friend from grade school at St. Mike's, had taken off in an antique Cadillac summoned for the occasion from a wrecker's graveyard. They were headed for Jacob's uncle's rustic cabin on Higgins, one of Michigan's larger inland lakes, known for endless quantities of bluegill and algae, surrounded by go-kart tracks and putt-putt courses. In other words, the perfect ironic honeymoon spot for a wedding intent on irony.

Nina was sitting on Earl's bed, and Toby was kissing her. Sloppy-tongued open-mouthed drunken kisses.

Most of them had lived variously together and apart at Alba in what was affectionately known as the Brown House. Most of them couldn't say for sure who was living there at any given moment. That was almost the point of the Brown House. Except for Toby—they made no mistake about inviting Toby to live there.

Nina's boyfriend Larry had fallen asleep in one of the two matching orange easy chairs near the windows overlooking the parking lot. Larry was a heavy sleeper. At a Brown House party the previous year, Earl had been the one kissing Nina while Larry slept. Then, they'd gotten up and gone into Earl's room on the second floor and had drunken frenzied sex, and when they came back down, Larry was still blissfully out while the music throbbed and people danced around them. Everybody loved good ol' Larry.

Bliss had always seemed like a simple uncomplicated kind of happiness to Earl, a happiness he did not feel when having sex with Nina, or certainly not now, watching Toby kiss her. Was bliss even possible, when every decision felt like a leap into thin air with all the consequences of landing without a net?

Earl grabbed a cold beer from the watery wastebasket they'd loaded with ice hours ago. He wanted to sleep, but his bed was occupied. He was occupied with thoughts of Rita, who, in his future fantasies, was supposed to be his bride—just some day, not now. They were close—close enough for near-bliss on blue-moon nights when their helium-balloon planets created beautiful friction and high-pitched satisfaction, or on nights when they were simply both desperate and drunk enough to plow through the borders of their deep friendship and nourish their secret night-flower into blossom.

A small part of him, based on situation and proximity, wished he was kissing Nina again. Why had she stayed with Larry, and what would they do next, together or apart? Larry was from Marquette in the U.P., Nina was from Shepherd north of Alba, and they were spending the summer together in the Brown House where rent was cheap, almost nonexistent, when the students were gone.

They were trying to sort it out. Kissing at a party had consequence now—beyond the exchange of bodily fluids—weight, repercussions. They were all driving off in the morning, scattering away from Detroit on the lifelines up the palm after one more breakfast together at Brays Bellybusters across the parking lot. No getting together in the fall to compare notes, to slink and sink into the comfort zone of college time, a time zone consisting of less daylight and more night, less accountability and oversight, more and more delay, one endless incomplete of a time.

At graduation, it had been all "see you at the wedding," so the buildup had been unsustainable, and the letdown inevitable. The after-party was a last-gasp effort to make some kind of imprint or addendum or secret watermark to their years together at Alba. They seemed to be taking it out on each other.

Earl stood near the door watching. They had a block of rooms at the end of the motel, and friends were spilling over into the hallway, crowding the corner. In the tiny room, someone jostled Larry and ended up in his lap.

Larry stirred, then put his thick hand firmly on Toby's shoulder. Nina pushed Toby away. "I think that's enough," Larry said.

"Yeah, I guess so," Nina said. She wiped saliva off her face and flung back her hair, as if she'd just defeated Toby in a wrestling match. Toby looked sheepish, Earl thought, and it was not a good look for him. It wouldn't be a good look for him as a P.E. teacher at Alba High where he'd start in the fall, having wrestled there in high school. Even when Toby was not accepted at any of the seventeen law schools he applied to, he had not looked sheepish.

Earl thought it was enough too. He had to get up in the morning and drive to work for his morning shift at Chrysler Assembly to pick up some overtime. He'd promised his father he'd go back to the factory if he didn't find anything in his field, whatever that was.

He didn't want to observe the fallout from the caught kissers, so he walked out the door and down the hallway and stairs to the first floor and approached the front desk.

"There's a loud party in—" he took his room key out to look at it—"in Room 214. Can you ask them to break it up?"

The young desk clerk—a recent graduate or dropout of Eight Mile High, Earl guessed—sullenly got to his feet. "Yes, sir, I'll take care of it."

Earl walked around the corner and out the side door into the parking lot. Soft, warm June night, nearly perfect for the final scene in the movie of the first part of his life. Wind blew through his thin, white shirt still damp with sweat from dancing, or from the hot air of his best friends. He shivered. Fluorescent floodlights glowed at regularly spaced intervals onto cars parked at slightly odd angles against the rigidity of the yellow-lined spaces. He would wait out here while the young clerk did his job. One light flickered, faintly abuzz, and he trained his eyes on that.

4. Notes on the Facts

No facts, only rumors of facts, like bed bugs down at the Suez Motel. Are they really there? Are they specks of guilt for what you did or didn't do?

———————————

When you're young, Consequence is the name of a street miles away in an upscale subdivision. Nothing to do with your life on the crumbling edge of Eight Mile Road. Sleeping with your best friend seems like some bonus prize to a trick question you guessed the answer to in a random accident.

———————

No such thing as a random accident.

———————

We can't agree on even the most basic facts, lost in the foggy memory-blur of wishful breezes.

———————

"Remember, you were my date at Gene's wedding. What's-her-name had just vaporized, and . . ."

"I have no memory of that."

"The bridesmaids wore these stupid chiffon hats that we mocked all night?"

———————

What I didn't say in front of Jake: "Then I took you home and we screwed on your living room couch while your parents slept above us in your old house on Archangel Street."

———————

Did she really not remember? When did she start seeing Jake? I was supposed to be marrying what's-her-name two months later. We started in on the already-purchased cases of liquor in my father's basement, but we didn't get very far. I think Jake and I drove over to her house and threw up on her front lawn. Or maybe we just rested there on her parents' perfect green square of grass and discussed the meaning of life.

True love is like an ink eraser. Remember those?

———————

Eight Smiles Road. Eight Miles High. Ate my sky. Bar? High school? Border?

Love triangles are a neat simplification of complex relationships. Lines never equal in length. Never the hardened perfection of a pyramid. But in Earl's case, it was more like parallel lines. The line between Jake and Rita, paved, with firmly painted yellow lines and groomed shoulders, point A to point B. In a parallel universe, a dotted line of sparse gravel connected Earl and Rita. A meandering trail—overgrown in places, rutted in places. Old winter salt still trying to melt ice in other places. Stones kicked to the curb. Crossed wires. Shorts. Sparks. Expired fire extinguishers rusted to the walls.

I am part Earl, but not all Earl. As I look back, I become more Earl. I have a fondness for Earl. When I talk about my past, I tell stories about Earl as if they were true and happened to me.

Detroit had a leak in the overpass that dripped on to the pedestrian tunnel below Eight Mile. In winter, the drips froze into ice in the tunnel. Instead of fixing the drips, they fenced off the part of the tunnel where the ice formed.

When I think of Jake, I picture him stumbling down the steps, drunk and naked, and tripping over my younger sister sleeping in the hallway on his way to take a leak after one of the legendary Brown House parties. Not every time I think of Jake. Just the times when I think about how I betrayed our friendship.

The baby is Jake's. I think that was pretty certain all along. That other baby exed out in photos, that baby is mine.

————————

The Suez advertised their prices on the plastic sign out front like Mc-Donald's advertised the number of burgers sold. Like the sign on I-94 advertised the number of new cars built each year until they, the Big They, decided it was better not to document the diminishing numbers, better not to remind the ex-workers driving rust buckets down the freeway how screwed they were.

It started at $19.95 a night. Only one way to go from there.

————————

Fun fact: Earl spent the night before the wedding in a hotel room with the groom on three separate occasions, and all those weddings ended in divorce. Tip: have Earl make his own hotel arrangements.

————————

Couples from Alba exchanged vows in various denominational ceremonies and celebrated in a wide range of identical ethnic wedding halls across the state while everyone else was building lofts, shacking up, not changing their names, and where was Steve/I mean Earl/I mean Dick/or Harry but in the middle, changing point of view once again, talking about himself in the third person to escape the shame of getting left behind somewhere on the freeway, like when his car broke down on the ramp when he was giving Willie Warren a ride back to Detroit and he thought Willie was his friend even though he was black because they grew up within a few miles of each other. Willie simply got out of the car and walked away with his thumb out, taking his chances with other white drivers in the middle of the mitten, taking his chances as he did every day just by being one of the few black students at Alba. Earl didn't understand that then. All he understood was his own deep and profound abandonment, a double cheeseburger of self-pity and a greasy bill from the tow-truck driver who could tell he wasn't from around there and priced himself accordingly.

Willie, the only black person in the story. Why? Because Eight Mile? Because Alba? Because Earl? Ahmed Aditya comes back all the way from Ethiopia to make a brief appearance and ask, why wasn't I invited to the wedding?

Ahmed and I once had a heated argument about whether spaghetti grew on trees. Ahmed and Willie were not friends. "He's from Ethiopia, dude," Willie said. "Detroit. Ethiopia. I have more in common with you white motherfuckers than some dude from Ethiopia."

Carried by a tide of dead brain cells, the Polish Century Club may have migrated over from Outer Drive to Eight Mile and turned into a wedding party instead of my friend Harry's high school graduation party. I had been on the wagon after streaking through a Big Boy's restaurant, much to everyone's chagrin. Even the larger-than-life statue of Big Boy blushed with shame or fury. It was the first time I heard anyone use chagrin in a sentence. I was chagrined not to remember much about that night, though the details were readily available in the hallways of Eight Mile High.

I went off the wagon, though kept my clothes on. I slept it off in a barber's chair or dentist chair in somebody's basement. My worst nights end up in anonymous basements.

Being the life of the party was a matter of opinion. *Life* could mean *village idiot*. At Eight Mile High, given the value placed on self-destructive behavior, it took a lot to be the village idiot—many competitors, and some of them, like Denny and Buzz Smolinski from down on Mound Road, became our "Usual Suspects" before blossoming into long-term convicts. Denny and Buzz—see, I had to use those names . . .

Given the circumstances, given the willingness to shun all possible consequences, Earl could have and had done many things he would come to regret—Regret, the place that, when you go there, it has to take you in.

Nirvana was Earl's dog's name. A dog he abandoned in a field near farmland hoping someone would adopt him. He opened the door of his pickup, and Nirvana jumped down.

Earl slammed the door and sped off, and in his rearview mirror he watched Nirvana running behind him, disappearing as the road curved. When he tells this story, he pretends someone else did it.

Everyone knows the wings melt. What happens to Icarus when he falls into the sea? Legend has it—well, it's all legend, but the story goes that his body washed ashore and Hercules recognized him. But maybe he was a good swimmer. Maybe he made underwater friends and married a selkie.

Exactly how far does the Road Runner run over the cliff's edge before he looks down and begins to fall?

Before Rita looks back at the K of C door to see Earl disappear into the night and they both turn into pillars of salt?

We have to go back to the wedding and study the photos. We have to light the last match in the wedding matchbook from back when everyone smoked. Jake and Rita, June 5, 1981. Light it, then blow it out, then make a wish.

Earl's lighting up in the parking lot. He rarely smoked dope alone. Angus was always game and didn't force conversation. He was a smiling stoner, and that smile was enough. But tonight, outside the Polish Century

Club—the Italian Decade Club, the Irish Millennium Club, he could be anywhere without Rita—watching late-night Michigan license plates whoosh past on the road to perdition. The road to sleep. The road of clear decisions.

He knew enough to not want to be married, even after the big dramatic production of what's-her-name following him to Alba—they broke up, got engaged, then broke up again. He acted all broken-up about it for months longer than he needed to. Truth was, if he'd gotten serious with Rita, they would have cheated on each other. Or, if it wasn't the truth, he took satisfaction in imagining it could be—because he'd never know.

If Earl was really going to simply burn his wings and walk off into the night like a rebel without a cause, leaving Archangel Street behind once and for all, mixing his metaphors into a toxic self-pitying stew, now was the time.

But the DJ was playing his song (his secret song), and nobody was missing him inside as the party rocked on, so in this version he's going to do one thing right and go back inside and dance his ass off.

Some names have been changed to convict the innocent. Others have overlapped, stuck in the unlocked revolving door of the Brown House where people came and went in odd increments so it was nearly impossible to tell exactly who was living there at any given time. The owner of the house, Rex Hazzard, the closeted gay lawyer who lived next door—may he rest in peace—had written no lease since he was an honorable man who built his world around love and trust and is still mourned by many.

———

If this were a true story, Earl would've slept with way too many of the guests at this wedding, given the times, the great pre-AIDS sexual awakening, which had its problems and complications, but which many think was still a pretty cool time to come of age.

———

Was he more irritated by not being able to go to sleep after a long, strangely stressful day, rather than by Toby kissing Nina? He half-felt like waking up good ol' Larry just to stir things up and get them out of his room.

———

When what's-her-name moved into the Brown House the following year with the guy she ended up marrying, that stung, but not as much as he thought it would. Earl was glad to be gone, just like he'd been glad to be clear of Eight Mile High when he first escaped to Alba. He wasn't sure how many fresh starts life allowed, but he was hoping for a few more stashed away in his savings account under his pillow.

———

Was there even a honeymoon? Earl couldn't remember. All he knows is he went in to work and stumbled through another day of welding axle housings together. At the end of summer, there'd be no returning to the Brown House. The next time he makes it to Alba, the house will be repainted a dark green with a Mexican family sitting on the porch staring stoically at him as he cruised slowly past in Rex's funeral procession. Yes, AIDS even reached the Middle of the Mitten. I pulled a reverse double-whammy with the lightning strike killing him.

———

Earl hoped he'd get laid off at the end of the summer. Rita had an abortion in Canada, the abortion capital of Michigan. She and Jacob moved west to California (in California, he was Jacob). Earl had passively hoped that Rita would still be around when he was ready to settle down. Dumbass.

———————

The Brown House crowd found itself spread out across various tables in the hall in haphazard pairings that seemed like pure whimsy, as if they'd stuck all their names on a dartboard and taken their shots. Earl was by himself, so they'd placed him next to Rex Hazzard. Rex was so poorly named that they'd tried out a variety of nicknames for him, but nothing stuck. He was not a Rex, or a hazard. He introduced himself as Rex, almost apologetically. His closest friend and perhaps secret lover was a Catholic priest. Soft-spoken and considerate, Rex acted in productions by the Gratiot County Players and lawyered for the local oil company. He had an autographed photo of the famous oil-fire fighter Red Adair on his office wall.

Earl wanted to be named Rex Hazzard. A running joke. A running hazard.

———————

Everything else is human life, and that's too complicated.

———————

Earl didn't like watching other people kiss.

———————

"I guess congratulations are in order then, buddy," though he'd already filled that order multiple times in the past few weeks.

———————

Earl studied the room, the older couples quietly eating—his friends' parents and aunts and uncles and two unrelated surviving grandparents.

How might it feel to be together that long, aging flesh thinning beneath their unchanging golden rings?

I have a fondness for Earl.
  I have a fondness for Rita.

Maybe she did have the baby.
  Named Lettie, after Rita's mother, the singing waitress.

One drunken night years later, we burned the rocket ship in Rita's backyard—against some law, I'm sure. The Eight Mile cops cruised past slowly, perhaps concerned about the trailer park, a place they visited regularly. I guess it looked like we had everything under control. Rita and I and her good-for-nothing stoner brother Brad, who had emerged from some gutter after getting a whiff of cash money. They were selling the house before it completely collapsed. None of us had any performance art left in us. Jake had taken off alone, splashing down in a safe zone in a southern state that had the word North in it.

Truth is, the night wasn't drunken at all.

I know it's not enough to let people know who wins. When it comes down to it, does anyone ever really win? Not for very long. Important to shuffle the pieces so people care, even though we all know the house wins. Right, Jake?
  Every time I count the cards, I get a different total. I'm not much of a gambler anymore, so that doesn't surprise me. I'm a passenger on a lot

of wagons. My hands are folded more often than not these days—not in prayer, but in something else I might never figure out.

———————

I've got one more little story here that I've been holding onto. The hole card of the cheater at solitaire. No need to hide it, but still . . .

5. Christmas Story Addendum

No ace in the hole, and that'll be my last card metaphor. I hold onto this story for its bittersweet flavor that pulls me right back to Eight Mile Road. I feel it in my throat on days my heart rises up at odd, surprising moments. I savor it, even as it hurts when I swallow it back down. Stings my nostrils. Pricks my skin.

Nobody's getting married. Nobody's hurting anybody else today. I'm at my folks' house, living in the basement—which I did for a couple of decades off and on. The basement, where, when you go there, they have to open the heat vent in the rafters.

December, pre-Christmas, and Rita calls. Late morning, but I'm still asleep, hungover, as I often was over a couple of decades off and on. My mom doesn't care. She hollers down the stairs: Phone Call!

Rita wants to know if I'll help her pick out a Christmas tree. "I don't want to do it alone," she says. Out of the blue, though no blue exists in gray December skies in Detroit. Grays create the blues, and we both had them.

———————

I slumped gratefully into her car. I usually got drunk on beer or cheap wine, but the holidays called for doing shots—or, more specifically, a group of Eight Mile friends had called for the shots, friends that went for the hard stuff, year round, unlike me, the college boy. No saying *no* to those guys—one of the reasons I ended up at Alba in the first place, thinking it'd be my little monastery in the middle of Michigan, smaller than my high school, with some vague religious affiliation. A dry-out camp for drunks like me.

The short version is that I learned quickly that a nonbeliever in a monastery is still a nonbeliever.

"Hey," Rita said. Her car smelled vaguely of pot and patchouli, which I suppose did not make her distinct from a whole range of young women back then, but I always associate it with Rita.

"Hey," I said back. Chrysler Imperial. Bigger than she needed, but that was just the Detroit multiplier—everybody had a car bigger than they needed. Bench seat in the front. She bent her head to get a good look at me.

"How ya doing? Rough night?"

I hadn't eaten anything yet. I had that taste in my mouth, the stupid taste. I groaned for a lack of a better word or words.

We got stoned enough so that I was almost feeling human again. She took me to Brays Bellybusters, our local equivalent of White Castle, for the 6 burgers/$1.50 special. I was in Brays once when this guy who had a knife sticking in his side asked the grill cook to call 911, then sat down at the long aluminum counter. Someone bought him a coffee that he sipped while waiting for the ambulance.

I wanted to say it was me who bought his coffee, but I can't lie like that in a story about Rita. We based our whole friendship on not lying to each other. At Alba, it was an unspoken pact between us, the two white-trash representatives/refugees/rebels without a cause from Eight Mile High to maroon ourselves there.

By the time we got to the tree lot—an old used-car joint rearranged with trees and littered with dry needles—the sun had, against all odds, emerged, turning the sky a blue you had to squint up into and believe in.

An unshaven older man, whiskers blotched gray in spots, wearing a shabby green jacket repaired with a crudely sewn blue-jean patch, sat on a stool leaning against the abandoned shack of the used-car dealer. Apparently, his arrangement with whoever owned the lot now did not include a key to get inside. Nobody wants to sit outside for hours in Detroit in December. Even the drunken ice fishermen on the Detroit River have their forlorn porta-potty-sized shacks.

"I don't think he's working on commission," I said as we got out of the car. If you've never gotten stoned in a car in winter, then stepped outside into cold sunshine, I highly recommend it. The pure cold rushes up your nose and you feel briefly awakened, as if the car door created a vacuum when you opened it, and everything loose and buoyant got sucked toward you.

That's how I remember it. Maybe it depends on who you're with.

I used to correct people—or think I was correcting people—on their memories, but memories don't need correction, I've finally learned. What fun would it be if we all remembered everything the same way? What fun would it be if we couldn't make shit up and add it to memory like fertilizer?

Rita, she's squinting and smiling this crooked little smile that any random stranger might fall in love with, even old Gruffy McDuff on his stool—one of those overturned five-gallon white buckets, I see, as we approach his scowl.

I too am among the unshaven. I too would have matched his scowl if it hadn't been for the telepathic morning phone call from Rita.

Did I tell you she was a telepathy major?

Did I tell you they tore down the Brown House to widen West Center Street and made it one way to create a little loop down Main Street the other way, for no apparent reason, since Main Street is dying, every other storefront boarded up due to the Wal-Marting of America that's even kicked K-Mart's ass down the road?

What are we gonna do? We're gonna buy a goddamn Christmas tree from this old chain-smoking geezer who's already marked his territory with cigarette butts spiked in the snow around him like dud firecrackers.

We don't like those spikey scotch pines, even though they're cheap. We pick a balsam fir—scraggly, but they smell great once you get them inside. Rita's parents are on borrowed time, and Rita's paying the interest on that time to keep them alive. Her father's last Christmas at home.

"Do you ever get monks and monkeys mixed up?" I asked.

"No, EJ, I don't," she said.

In addition to that smile, that was another thing that made me love Rita: she still called me EJ—okay, dumb nickname, but it's what they called me at Eight Mile, and she called me that at Alba as part of our private code. When she called me EJ, a door opened and the warm light of her house on Archangel Street came rushing in. I wish that she'd had a nickname in high school, but I don't recall one. Sometimes I sang her name in "The Name Game" song, but that didn't count for much, since just about everybody knew it. That, and "The Clapping Song." God bless Shirley Ellis.

"Them balsas smell nice," the man said, helping me tie it to the roof of Rita's car reflecting gold in that sudden, sustained miraculous sunshine. Even the snow was melting a little, creating dark puddles that drained into the sewers along Eight Mile Road. We could see the laughing, spinning donkey on the top of Brays Bellybusters holding up a giant burger on one of his hooves, and a milk shake on the other. Cash only, to this day.

"Hey, I just figured something out," I said. It was like the rough hand of God shook me with a deep insight into the meaning of life. You idiot, God was saying.

"The reason they got a donkey up there is because of the name—Brays—get it, donkeys bray!"

"Where did you get this dim-widget," the guy said, yanking the rope tight, then cutting it with a large and perhaps illegal switchblade.

Rita laughed, and the man laughed, and I, who had never been called a dim-widget, also laughed.

The guy held a dirty roll of cash in one hand. I gave him the bills from my wallet, and he added to his wad. With all that cash, he was the perfect customer for Brays. The Bellybuster was their double-decker hamburger, though truth be told, any burger from Brays was likely to bust your belly. I do not recall an apostrophe, though it should have one in case somebody's named Bray out there: Bray's, the house of Bray.

"You're such a sweet couple," he said as we did the exchange. Fishing for a tip, we all knew. "You look like newlyweds. Is this your first Christmas together?"

Oh, man, the way Rita blushed, and me, I could feel my face flushing too. If somebody knows how to stop a face from turning red, don't tell me. It's one of those pure things left that I hope scientists don't have a bead on yet.

I wasn't much of a tipper then, and perhaps I am not to this day. Tipping wasn't part of our repertoire, nor was the word repertoire. We never ate out along Eight Mile Road, or at Alba, except in altered states of late night/early morning. It made us squirm to have anybody serve us. I could go on about tipping, but I'll just admit I am a cheapskate, a word we used with confidence and comfort. Makes it even more of a miracle that I paid for Rita's tree and gave the guy an extra buck.

A man with a dirty wad of bills in his pocket, flipping out your change with greasy fingers, is someone you should probably trust. At that point, it's too late to do anything about it anyway.

———————

The closest we'd ever come to marrying, and I suppose that's not very close. But getting married in a rutted used-car lot by an escapee from Carney-ville in sight of Brays would've been the perfect spot. Even better than her parents' backyard, where she married Jake in front of the plywood Rocket Ship.

———————

She remembers it differently.

———————

My grandfather lived in a wooden house in Detroit nearly his entire life. Painted it yellow. Easy to find—not a lot of yellow houses on Harding Street in Detroit. Particularly after nearly every other house on the street was burned or torn down during the tough years of Devil's Night arson and crack houses. He chained his rocking chair to the rotting porch through a hole he'd drilled in the crawl space beneath. We left that rocker swaying in the wind when we moved him out and abandoned the house to the elements.

The Brown House looked a lot like the Yellow House, but we never chained up our rocking chair or even locked the door. I lived in that house for two years and never had a key. None of us did, remember, Rita? I would've kept the key if I ever had one.

———————

My grandfather worked as the handyman for the church across the street until they gutted the church—St. Rose of Lima—and tore that down too. When they tear down your memories, you have to remember harder, or just let them blur and take whatever shape they're going to take.

The priest, Father Raymond, was an advocate for the poor who personally delivered donations across the city, with his sidekick driver, my grandfather. Which is why one day my grandfather carried a full-sized harp, the kind they play in heaven, across the street from the church and into his front hallway.

He didn't want to see it tossed in the trash. Just like he didn't want to throw away his empty milk jugs, but that's another story down the long wobbly road. I don't know how he got that harp in the front door. The scale of it was ridiculous if you stood next to it in his tiny foyer. Most of the strings were broken or missing, but a few remained.

That day we moved him out to the demilitarized zone of a tiny, tiny house near Nine Mile and Mound, I stood in that hallway—my grandfather did not want to leave, but we were making the move in one trip, knowing it was the only trip we had, since once the truck pulled away, it would be anyone's ballgame on Harding's rubbled field. We'd already had the power turned off.

I plucked one thick string hard, and it thrummed and echoed in the silence of my grandfather standing hands on hips and holding back tears.

Like it sounds in heaven. Like a long blushing moment in a used-car lot with a giant donkey looking down on us, as we caught each other's eyes and held.

Watching *Blow Out*

The lone usher marched down the aisle to order us to put our feet down. My friend Earl and I, the only ones in the place. I'd helped him move to Pittsburgh from Detroit. Earl and me, his pal Oscar, at the movies—our old friend, darkness, following us to Pittsburgh. We'd carried his girlfriend Claire's stuff up three flights of stairs, assuming she'd soon follow. An assumption that would benefit only U-Haul. I'd left my wife Marie for Gail, a younger version of Marie who liked sex in public places, who then left me for no one at all, so I was sitting pretty low in my seat. I'd sold Earl a quarter pound of pot at the family rate—starter kit for his new city—and I was happy to roll it up and light joint after joint across the Ohio turnpike. The movie was *Blow Out*, by Brian De Palma. I remember only the large nipples of a young actress. My life was listing, taking on water. My feet were up to keep them dry. That usher's enormous flashlight sent us back to getting kicked out of *Ben-Hur* at the Bel-Air Theater on Eight Mile after our local bully Denny Smolinski sat down next to us and threw Jawbreakers at some girls till the usher dragged the three of us out. Smolinski didn't care—bored, even by *Ben-Hur*. His father kicked his ass, and Smolinski kicked everybody else's. Earl and I silently glowered into that bright sunshine of a wasted Saturday afternoon. Denny threw his last handful of candy at us as we edged away. Red Hot Dollars, the coin of his realm. That usher in Pittsburgh wouldn't kick us out of an empty theater. We sat through the final half-hour, our feet obediently lowered. Who was that woman with the large nipples? Maybe I needed to smoke another joint. Maybe I needed to move to Pittsburgh myself. We returned to his attic apartment's pent-up heat. He didn't even have a fan, signing the lease in May, not anticipating summer. Perhaps she had anticipated not being there. I had failed to anticipate a lot of things, so I sweated it out with him until the next day when I drove the empty U-Haul back to Detroit, feeling the weight of all that emptiness holding me back. Years after she dumped me, I tracked down Gail, sent a long letter recalling all the small details of our public and private time together. This was after I remarried and had two kids. I was blowing up old nude photos of Gail in my blacked-out bathroom. Gail called Earl to beg him not to tell me where she was. Back then, walking out of *Blow Out* into another Saturday squint, Earl did not anticipate sleeping on the floor for six months, waiting for Claire, then waiting for her only to come get all her stuff. My help was not requested. No blow out—just a slow leak from her vein—but that small hole led to free-fall. I speak from experience. I translate addiction. I talk in the tongues of addiction. Russian immigrants lived on Earl's first floor. We passed them dozens of times unloading the truck, and they said not a word. Based on their decorating scheme, they believed in UFOs and Jesus. I believed in old nude photos and the blessings of darkness. I heard them below us that night, guilt rising up through the floorboards. I slept with Claire and gave her drugs back in Detroit. In March, she finally left for Pittsburgh with an empty U-Haul—with that leak in her arm, she needed little else. I kissed her bruised forearms while she slept the night before she left. She was living with me for my stuff. She returned in a crammed U-Haul in a brutal snowstorm and landed on some other planet or star or black hole that wasn't mine. *Blow Out* in a dark, empty, mall multiplex. What could I say about anyone's new life? I found a dark theater. I sat, waiting. The candy rained down on me.

The Perp Walk

Somebody's gotta do the perp walk or the breakup's not official. Is stuff exchanged? If there's no exchange of stuff, it's not official, just a fling. You don't break up from a fling.

Claire and I'd lived together a number of months—double-figure months, maybe a year—above the Powder Puff lingerie store at 525½ Ashville, a small side street off Eight Mile Road behind Eight Miles High, a dive bar that hid its cue sticks for the safety of all concerned.

During that time, we made as much noise as those two birds squabbling in my tree out front at this very moment here in Pittsburgh. My tree, damn it—why don't those birds get a room above the Powder Puff back in Detroit?

Mrs. Puff didn't even notice. Or maybe we just kept different hours and did our squabbling after they closed/after a few drinks/after a couple pills from the pill drawer/after all customers buying underwear had gone home to put it on/to take it off/to live their powder-puffery lives.

Oh, man, all those important things I once wanted back I've now forgotten or abandoned or given away to Goodwill, having lost all good
will long ago.

For years, I carried around a scrap of paper itemizing all the money
Claire owed me in case . . . in case . . . she made a ton of money or wanted
to make amends? Or even reunite? I wasn't sure—that list, the only thing
I had left after the tiny TV she'd inherited from Gino, an earlier ex, then
left behind with me (double breakup hoodoo!) blew up during the Oscars
one year, emitting smoke and a toxic stench before they'd even given
away the supporting actor award.

I'd stuck the rabbit ears out the window up in the attic apartment
I lived in after moving out of the second-floor apartment Claire and I
were supposed to have shared. After I explained the situation, Manny,
the landlord, the King of Sighs, sighed, then said I could move up to the
third floor. She'd signed the lease! She never moved in! After we lugged
all her stuff from Detroit in a U-Haul in August! I found myself staring
into Manny's giant pores in his giant nose.

"To tell you the truth [sigh], I thought she seemed a little wacko when
I met her that one time." Manny chewed cigars but didn't smoke them
anymore: "The wife [sigh]. What can you do?"

Oh, we were excited signing that lease together with Manny sitting
across from us at his orange kitchen table—like the night we got drunk
at Eight Miles and decided to get married in the morning, went back to
Puffville, took a couple hits of speed to keep us up, then called everyone
we knew to tell them the great news and even called a priest to ask him
to perform the ceremony.

The priest—Father Frank—needed to be as strung out as we were
in order to make that happen, but we'd woken him up. He had mass in
the morning at St. Mike's. He and I took turns dropping our respective
phones, then he said, "Call me back when you're sober," but I never did.

Claire and I had gotten most everyone out of bed till she fell asleep cradling the receiver like it was her favorite doll or action figure.

I should've known she wasn't a follow-througher when she abandoned stripping and refinishing her green dresser in the middle of the third drawer. Two-and-a-half drawers looked great. The rest, probably still that pale, pukey green.

It was so unlike her to not inhale something that got her high. I myself occasionally took a whiff of the stripper, then returned to my own project, selling my old baseball cards to serious collectors who often disagreed with me on their condition. The difference between mint and near mint was as big as the difference between Claire signing the lease and her actually moving in. For years, I put too much faith in scraps of paper and not enough in human nature. Too much faith in keeping track and not enough on forgiving debts, real and imagined.

She took the dresser back to Detroit. What a story that dresser could tell, half-stripped, half-abandoned—moving out on a cold, rainy, gray March day [What did *you* do over spring break, kids?] after loading up U-Haul #2, after two days of sharing all the drugs we could lay our hands on—uppers, downers, in betweeners, whatever might get us through the unpacking and packing of our odd life together. Two days of endless dashes and a complete lack of sentence structure: *What if—? So what—? So, what?* The old Russian couple on the floor below us first politely knocked, then screamed at us in Russian to shut the fuck up. Claire told me she had a yeast infection, so we couldn't screw.

"Why tell one more lie at this point," I asked.

"Exactly," she said. "It's true."

Take more drugs and call me in the morning—or better yet, the after-noon—our prescription for everything. We hoarded pills. We lied to every doctor along Eight Mile Road, and three more out in the suburbs—it was worth the trip. The trip was our concern, not the destination. Thus, the lease was equal to the drunken promise to marry. That promise got us free drinks and a twelve-pack to go from Eight Miles before we left, but no speed was strong enough to keep us—or Father Frank—awake, to keep our mad dreams of sobriety at bay.

"Hey, at least it was better than *I'm going to kill myself*," we told every-one the next day when they called us back either pissed off or curious to see if we'd followed through. Mostly, just pissed off.

Are *you* getting pissed off? Wondering, hey, what about that breakup? Cameras flashing, TV crew chasing us, as we covered our faces [which one of us did the perp walk? Do you care?] with our jackets and scam-pered to the car, *no comment, no comment.*

I got her pregnant once! This is true! Suddenly, we were telling the truth to doctors. She carried around her cracked diaphragm as evidence in its nice protective plastic case. I had to drive from Detroit to Windsor, crossing borders with the currency of my lies. She'd fled the Puff in the middle of the night and in the morning called me up from Canada. Why was she so choosy about abortion clinics? [See, I could be a real asshole] [I'm suddenly fond of brackets all these years later] [more substantial than parens, railings I can hold onto to get up the stairs] [bad knees, and it's not from praying]. Hey, at least I drove over there—didn't mail it in. We could've gone together and saved time and gas money, I couldn't resist telling her. Resisting had never been my strong suit, my ace in the hole, my king of hearts.

She had a friend in Windsor she trusted. She didn't trust me. We split the cost of the procedure, plunking down the stiff, colored bills adorned with somebody's queen, then drove in a two-car caravan back to Michigan, and carried on as before, accumulating debts and the usual resentments. The usual debts and accumulating resentments.

The only time she showed no hesitation. In my memory, she was drunk the whole trip, and I was the sober, consoling presence (when not tossing Molson's bottles out the window of my Plymouth Satellite onto random Canadian lawns) as we drove around talking things over. In my memory, I tried to talk her out of it. Though we were broke. Broken. We'd misstepped. We were mistaken. Her friend in Canada didn't trust me either. She'd hung up on me that night we were getting married. Fuck you, she might have said on both occasions—all those fuck you's blend together after awhile. Memory doing the perp walk. Getting lost on the way to the car. Dialing the wrong number. Car towed for an overdue phone bill? Busted by a priest with attitude?

———————

I carried around that scrap of paper in my wallet but said not a word while we packed U-Haul #2 and she drove off back to Detroit—well, she'd never really left. Detroit is a state of mind—flat, endless. They named the suburbs after illusions: Hills, Woods, Pointes. We invented our own landscape, building rolling hills out of recycled parking tickets and overdue bills.

———————

Had she gotten all new stuff, living alone for six months in Detroit, while I waited with her old stuff in Pittsburgh? She never even learned to spell Pittsburgh with an h. The mailman kept correcting her spelling on envelopes till I told him how much she owed me [she wrote letters after her phone got cut off].

She had a lot of old stuff. Baggage. More than me, and it made me strangely jealous. The bed was hers, and I wouldn't sleep on it. I threw couch cushions down and slept on the floor, thinking the discomfort might bring her back—some kind of Catholic logic, I guess.

When she returned for her stuff, we slept together in that bed, facing away from each other, her little butt bumping against my little butt while we dreamt of inventing Memory Foam. The bed, the last thing we packed in the U-Haul. We'd left room for it.

———————————

I think she planned on moving in with Oscar when she got back to Detroit. She'd called him long distance from what was now officially *my* apartment—who would pay for *that* call when the bill came? No more room on my scrap of paper. It all seems pitiful now, my faith in numbers, in writing things down. I should have been drawing cartoons instead. Little Bazooka Joe Zen-like cartoons on that weird waxed paper they used.

Perhaps she had already moved in with Oscar—I'm not sure how much stuff *he* had, but he had plenty of drugs. He'd been my dealer. I'd stocked up for the move, getting a nice supply and variety for us, but ended up taking all the drugs myself, which may have been what made sleeping on the floor so comfortable. I'd refused to send her drugs via the U.S. mail as she'd requested. Maybe she eliminated me as the middleman and got them gratis from Oscar.

Nice enough guy, that Oscar, but he didn't even get the TV! I got it—Gino's TV! Did you even know about Gino and his TV, Oscar, you idiot back-stabber? I should have never played on that drugged-out slo-pitch softball team with you. I should've never let you borrow my glove. That glove's on the list, Oscar. I've got a lot of softball left in this life! I loved her, Oscar. Despite or because of the drugs. [Sorry—I'm going to stop talking about drugs now.]

Sorry, I just looked out the window here in Pittsburgh and saw this brilliant volcanic sunset and had to call my wife Betty to look out and confirm its beauty. After living alone for many years, I don't trust my own eyes.

The next year, when I went back to Detroit, my friend Oscar narced me out [many variations on the spelling of narced—I don't think it gets written down much] and told Claire I was in town hanging out at Eight Miles, so she could find me. I was afraid of seeing her [see lack of impulse control].

By the way, how many of you have looked at the ass-end of a U-Haul driving away, then went back in the apartment or the house and threw up and cried or just sighed and turned on Gino's old black and white TV for the next 72 hours? U-Haul should give you a punch card—break up five times, get the next rental free. They should design special breakup vans and trailers with clever messages or scenes of Hawaiian waterfalls on them: *Bye-bye! Happy Trails! Die Like a Pig!*

She comes in to Oscar's apartment where I'm staying (thanks again, buddy) wearing that strapless purple dress she knew I liked, ridiculously easy to remove.

[We had great sex above the Powder Puff, I think. Or, at least ambitious. If they'd had Memory Foam back then, I might remember more of it.]

She's got a big pimple on her forehead—unusual, since she took such good care of her skin. Everything could be a mess, but her skin was always cleansed and moisturized. I can picture that plum face even now, her hands rubbing in cream like she was shining up a magic cocaine lamp.

I barely resisted the impulse to squeeze that zit—the impulse to touch her, to un-blemish her, had me twitching. August—no hiding from the heat in those ancient Mayflower apartments Oscar lived in after his wife Marie kicked him out because he was having an affair with Gail, the daring young trapeze artist who liked having sex in public places.

Marie had been committed to making it work after her botched early marriage to Gene, and had been thinking it was time to have a kid after ten years with Oscar, while Oscar was thinking it was time to screw around, so that wasn't going to end well, was it, Oscar? And then Gail, after Oscar's divorce, she's not so crazy about having sex with Oscar in an apartment like normal people—or with Oscar at all, really—so Oscar decides to mess up *my* life by tricking me into seeing Claire again. Oscar had seen Marie shopping at Valu Time with another guy—younger—and lost his mind in Frozen Foods, smashing his face in the bricks of spinach till he gave himself a nosebleed, so what was he thinking? [Fuck you, Oscar, by the way. Don't think I don't know.]

––––––––––––––

When I briefly started a new hobby of getting straight, I confessed to Father Frank later that year. Thought I'd go traditional Catholic and jettison some sins in a quick recap of the last few years. I reminded him of the phone call, thinking, well, that was a real cluster-fuck of sins. His ear moved away from the little window. A young, gay priest, and if anyone would've married us back then, it might've been him.

Frank had the sweetness of a guy who'd been picked on in school. Someone who aimed to please but whose aim was bad. I never went to confession again, though I've done even stupider things since then [see trading car for drugs]. He said to me, "Look, I'm not giving you any penance. You know what to do." And before I could respond, *what's that?* he slid my little window shut and shifted to the other side.

Confessionals were wired—when you knelt down, the light outside went on so nobody walked in on you. The safety of a public bathroom stall for relieving yourself. I understand they do things differently now—group confessions, silent confessions, public confessions—though I think breakups are pretty much the same, even with computers—a cyber perp walk is still a perp walk. Maybe even worse for being both invisible and more public. And no one, absolutely no one, gets in the last word.

Unlike Oscar, I've never had sex in a public restroom, but a confessional would have seriously interested me. Confessionals smell like sin—public bathrooms smell like someone tried to scrub away sin with chemicals and failed due to the overpowering smell of bodily functions. Confessionals smelled like the pure thought of sin released, the heavy breath of it, the half-regret of it. What percentage of sin were you truly sorry for? I'm 73% sorry for sleeping with Marie, Oscar's [ex]wife. And 27% unsure, since Marie and I had some history, he was screwing around on her to begin with, and Marie deserved better.

Because of her strapless purple dress, I knew Claire wasn't wearing a bra. I backed away from her hug. Maybe she wasn't wearing lingerie at all anymore since she de-Puffed and was living elsewhere—alone again, I was quick to learn. [She gave off that kind of sexual combustibility. Mid-afternoon, both of us hyper alert, aware of the ramifications and consequences of the slightest move or gesture.]

[*Powder Puff!* Sometimes just saying it makes me smile or grimace or get a hard-on or/Powder Puff/Powder Puff/Powder Puff!]

Oscar and I were taking one of those fantasy Kerouac-ish cross-country driving trips in his new car, a Mercury Montego purchased as a rebound maneuver—he'd just gotten officially divorced from beautiful Marie. They'd married young, succumbed to early onset boredom, etc. Too much TV? Not enough? Different friends? I'd hear about it in the car. *Why'd you tell Claire I was coming?* I'd ask. Did he know I hit on Marie again when he was in the limbo zone with Gail, thrilled by the possibility of someone walking in on them?

Claire managed to hug me anyway—I gave her a quick humped-over bump so I wouldn't feel her loose breasts. I'd never seen her cry, including when she got arrested and the cops gave her a black eye and a fat lip for attitude and she spent not one but two nights in jail. But she cried that afternoon.

To change the mood, I went into asshole mode—made fun of the headband, the zit—anything to stay out of bed with her—I'm like the illegitimate son Emily Dickinson never had, mad with these dashes— Emily would have put me up for adoption.

I had an emotional yeast infection [comparison wrong, just wrong, I know]. She shed silent tears. I still had that piece of paper in my wallet like an old rubber that never got used. Somebody's tears had smeared the numbers. I held myself tight against reaching for her. I offered her some of Oscar's stale bread sitting in an open plastic bag on the counter. She surprised me by taking a slice and nibbling at it. I'd quit drinking again. I didn't turn on the lights, so in the half-dark of late afternoon we said half-goodbyes. I did not look out the window at her perp walk. The purple dress, the slight swaying of those perky breasts in a spotlight of sun. [I guess I did look.]

But then I saw her again that night at the Eight Miles High bar. Claire and Oscar had conspired—she had me paged at the bar while we were out drinking before driving off the next day in the Montego. The bartender, who knew us both from our faux wedding night, seemed wryly amused when he shouted my name above the clamor and held up the phone. The twelve-pack to go had been a gift from him.

I was a Powder Puffer from way back. I don't even know what that means, but I feel compelled to say it. I picked up a female pro-am football player one night at the High, then ran into her months later at another bar—the Alibi?—and she grabbed me rough around the neck and held me.

"Do I know you?" she asked. She seemed relieved when I said no. I seemed relieved when she let go.

"You got me mixed up with someone else," I said. I had myself mixed up with someone else—my problem, and I'm still working on it.

I broke up with Claire after she'd already broken up with me, so we're even, right? No—I refused to get re-entangled, which was much different than loading up U-Haul #1 and driving across from MI across OH and into PA with my rat-friend Oscar, who liked to drive trucks and smoke dope. A simple solution, it seemed, but Oscar had a farting problem and plucked hairs out of his beard while he drove and chain-smoked Luckys unfiltered.

What's the world record for breaking up? How long? How many times? *Come over*, she'd shouted over the wry racket of EMH—it had many names but only one purpose. She said *I have a short thin spout*. Or more likely, *I want to sort things out*. I agreed to drive over to her new place on Nine Mile Road. Maybe breakups had progressive mile roads as well—but where did they end?

In the old days, she'd call me from places like Eight Miles High to say she was staying out. That meant she might not be climbing the stairs to 525½ Ashville Street that night. She could drink a table under the table. She had a knack for closing bars. What she did after that, I didn't want to know, but sort of did.

I didn't have to see her again that night, but I sort of did. I walked in her open screen door. She had a fan on—*my* fan, the little red plastic tabletop one. I'd forgotten about it. I could have used it up on the third floor of the King of Sigh's house back in Pittsburgh. She started explaining her complicated life, the jail time. Jail time! The robbery. The robbery! In return, I told her about Gino's TV exploding, while that little scrap of paper burned a hole in my wallet in the shape of the face of Jesus, like a prayer card, like a counterfeit promise, like your first hopeful, unrealistic wallet condom. When I think of her and money, I end up with condoms every time. Even now, I'm conjuring the U-O-Me list: phone bills, lost rent (well, that really wasn't lost—it was a runaway, that rent, and you could put up all the posters in the world up on telephone poles, but that rent wasn't coming home), the insurance, the help, those little bits of help. She was used to extra help. Her father, a Chrysler retiree, sent her a check every month [a secret from her mother].

Years later, a much bigger secret was revealed, and her father left her mother for a much younger woman and promptly died in her arms. Happy, by all reports, which means by *her* report, in a honest-to-goodness letter she sent out of the random blue blues of fake nostalgia for the Powder Puff days. I also got two random late-night phone calls spaced two years apart. And I also made three random late-night phone calls in one mad cluster. The breakup with Claire continues, though I've been married nearly half my life in fits and starts and ends. I have the same phone number/the same job I left Detroit for/the same nervous ticks/ but fewer of the same bad habits/I am a boring middle-aged mid-level safety-first guy. She is a campus cop (a cop!) at Purgatory University, something like that. I'm not sure how many times she's been married, or the circumstances (bar bet gone wrong?), though I know she once took someone else's name, which seems so unlike her that maybe I don't want to know more.

You can never give all the stuff back. You can never get all the stuff back. I probably gave her the damn fan, then forgot. Something about seeing it again, quietly rotating, was a body blow—I had to catch my breath, close my eyes, un-Puff myself from flashbacks of our time together, of that purple dress lying on the floor while the fan whispered across our naked flesh.

I did the final perp walk under her porch light. Oscar and I were getting an early start in the morning: California, there we'd went! I couldn't even finish my sentences until we were halfway to Nebraska, its own equally somber state of mind. *Getting an early start, etc.* No. We were getting a late start—too old and jaded for a California road trip in a Montego with standard transmission and no AC in August. We should have found someone younger and more eager to drive. We pooped out in a remote cocaine village in Colorado where Oscar's brother Beaver lived. Beaver had moved out west to attend the Famous Comedy Writer's School and soon got hired to teach there. He was the least funny human being on earth, even with all the free cocaine express-mailed from Oscar.

I tried to be polite to Claire, half-disappointed to no longer be in mad love with her. I'd always been good for a farewell fuck, to be crass about it—it made for a cleaner getaway. To remember you by. To forget you by. I'd done it before. I'd do it again. But a toxic tang hung in the air in the dim squalor of that tiny efficiency apartment [#3—no #1 or #2] in the long row of them carved out of old motel units. It dizzied me with panic, conjuring the chemical smell of that paint stripper she'd used on two and a half drawers—it could take your head off like crystal meth—and the smell of the baseball-card mafia guys with their cigars who waited forever one day at the door above the Puff so that I finally had to come out and get a face full of smoke as part of my education on the difference between near-mint mint and near mint.

Maybe I was just too sad. Because I really did love her once, Oscar. Her reckless everything—excess was her demon lover.

Demon lover? This shit's getting deep. But I have my adult boots on. I had an adult job in Pennsylvania where we spelled Pittsburgh with the H. Oscar and I originally planned the California trip when I had no adult job and was still drinking. Oh, I would start drinking again too—my hardest fucking breakup ever was with booze—but that, as they say, is the horns of the dilemma of another story.

I'd purchased my first pair of adult shoes for the job interview in Pittsburgh and promptly got enormous blisters on both feet just walking from the hotel to the office, proving that I was not yet ready for adult shoes. They hired me a month later after their first two choices turned them down, starting the stop-time funeral procession of U-Hauls that could only be seen at the time through the stoned vision of Oscar, who kept asking things like, "Now, why exactly isn't she moving in with you now?" And "So you think she's really coming? When?"

I realize I never explained why she didn't move with me in the first place. Why I lived with her stuff for months alone. I'm looking out the window—is the sunset giving off that odor? Is this the end of the world?

Her car, a rusty rust-colored Impala, needed work to make the drive. Her check hadn't cleared. It was a matter of timing. She had to finish up an incomplete. It was a matter of timing. Her younger sister Ellen was quitting the convent in favor of coming out as a lesbian. Her older sister was divorcing the largest drug dealer on Eight Mile [not you, Oscar]. It was complicated. It was a matter of timing. Her stuff was collateral. That's what I kept telling Oscar—why would she have us haul all this stuff out here if she wasn't planning on joining me?

The real Claire was somewhere in between the plan to get married and the plan to move to Pittsburgh with me—something inside kept driving her to jerk the needle from Full to Empty and back again. A thrill ride, and I'd purchased a fat roll of tickets, not understanding how those rides wear down, fall apart, and that the sleazy carnies are not to be relied upon, stealing your money and leaving town under cover of darkness.

Where was I? Dim squalor? The fan blew hot air on us in the odd kitchen-bedroom of that tiny box of an apartment, me at the desk chair, her on the counter top. I didn't bring up the move there and back, all those boxes up all those stairs, and how many—still unpacked—I could see from where I sat. Who knew the H made Pittsburgh hilly? I could look right up the short skirt of that purple dress and see her black panties. I didn't bring up how I couldn't sleep in the bed for all those months waiting for her, couch cushions scattered on the floor. Or the women I slept with on those cushions—I had regressed to watching the closing-time perp walks *in the dim squalor* of Pittsburgh bars—a walk of an entirely different pajama stripe—I was a paparazzi pickup artist, and shame on me.

Right when you think it's going to end, it doesn't end. A mad wind picks up behind you, blows you back into each other, the endless story of it. I never got used to standing up from the floor of that Pittsburgh apartment full of her dented milk crates and taped-up boxes—such a leap on nights when I was not alone, extreme disappearance of intimacy, suddenly taking in the whole scene like a helicopter shot in an action film. One sweet, kind, naïve woman said, *that was nice, can we do it again,* and I, who'd always said *yes,* even if I was drunkenly incapable, mumbled, *I don't think so,* and stumbled down the hall to the bathroom. Like I was still saving something for Claire just in case—that dusty mattress sagging against a wall in the next room behind the closed door.

I didn't want to look back, but even given a second chance not to, I still did, stepping off the one cracked safety-yellow cement step from Room/ Apartment #3 [the lawyer was the landlord/the landlord was the lawyer— unlike our quaint idyllic life in Puffville where no security deposit was required, even though Mrs. Puff called me Gino—it must have been easier to call us all Gino] and out of the range of the old-fashioned orange glow of her ancient porch light. My shoulders slumped with remorse, defeat, while on the verge of relief—exhilaration, even. She was holding the door open—torn screen dangling—letting bugs in, tears trickling down her face, silent tears like mine, for as I got into the darkness, they started streaming down my own face like a freak summer storm, another strong wind out of nowhere, and thunder, maybe even the dismal drum of hail.

But there was no storm, just tears, and the odd whimpers of those who had nothing left to say or give.

Sigh [still delusional, I fancy myself as the Prince of Sighs]. Sometimes I just want to disappear into one of Manny Rivers's giant pores and wait things out for a while. But I think Manny's dead. I lived in that house on Douglass with two S's for my first five years in Pittsburgh. I still—I'm afraid to admit—have the lease we signed together, our faux marriage license, in my strongbox. In my weakbox.

The house had three apartments, one on each floor. The third-floor efficiency was as cozy as I imagine Manny's pores to be, ceilings angling down over tiny rooms, welcoming caves of fetid heat in summer, breezy ice in winter, like any good attic. The claw-foot bathtub with the curtain on a circular rod surrounding it was my baptismal font. I made the sofa bed more comfortable by padding it with those couch cushions from the Danish Modern sofa I'd stolen from my parents years earlier. When I moved from the second floor to the third, I dragged the cushions up the stairs as part of the dowry for my single life.

———————

The mad Russians from the first floor eventually learned some English. They turned out to be UFO aficionados who slept under sheets of aluminum foil on special occasions like UFO holidays. When I finally moved out of 1797 Douglasssssss Avenue, I gave them my leftover foil. They think they're going to live forever. Good luck with that, Manny told them. Sigh. The Russians and I had some good talks before I left, and we signed an agreement about the thermostat setting [one thermostat for all three floors] at a table with Manny, who signed off on it too.

Aluminum foil has many uses, but reflecting alien rays did not seem to be one of them, nor deflecting the deep, heavy depression I fell into while sleeping on those couch cushions on the second floor and listening to the rambunctious love-making of the policewoman who lived on the third floor that turned my future sofa-bed into a rocker, the metal feet lifting up then crashing down as she had sex with whoever had clumped up all those stairs to be with her.

———————

When I moved to the third floor, I did not take the other thing Claire left [besides Gino's TV]—this incredibly heavy table she'd stolen with the help of Gino from the banquet facility where she was a hostess, the Polish Century Club on Eight Mile. A formidable table, the one where the Wedding Party sat. One night Gino borrowed a pickup, and he and a couple of his pals hoisted it into the truck bed and ran it out to the Puff, hoisting it up the rickety steps into Claire's apartment. Gino had some big friends, and they eventually helped him get into the restaurant business. No way was I getting that table up another set of stairs/no way was it going to magically bend around the narrow staircase to the third floor.

Claire had used it as a desk. One hell of a desk. A presidential fucking desk. I don't know what kind of wood it was—maybe cement wood. I carried it down those Puff steps with stoned Oscar and up the steps to Manny's [sigh] second floor with still-stoned Oscar, but she and I alone could not get it down the steps into U-Haul #2—we'd already done so much heavy lifting of drugs, we didn't have it in us. No room left. Room for the bed, but not the table with *Polish Century Club* stamped on the bottom, waiting for some best man to make a toast, waiting for the whole wedding party to climb up and do The Hustle on it because, damn, that table could take it. The bump, the swim, the mad boogaloo of the eternal tighten-up.

What's a Polish Century? A joke with a million punch lines.

I gave the table to the ex of someone I'd slept on the cushions with. Holly Wood, a local TV news anchor—her name was either an asset or a liability, according to her, depending on how much she'd had to drink. I could tell you a lot about that name, more than I care to know about anyone's name. She should have changed it [her birth name]. She was indeed from Los Angeles and claimed to have slept with Jim Morrison [not unusual, given The Lizard King's prodigious appetites. Sigh].

Holly owned a house with Harry Kizek. They had divided it into two apartments after they split up. The kind of compromise we learn to make when wearing our adult shoes [trust me, this all comes together at the end (I hope)]. They were still semi-friendly, though he wore no shoes at all. He was getting a PhD in Robotics so needed a sturdy table to create Frankenstein on. Since it was a Polish American table and he was Polish, he wanted it. He was a big guy who had hair but shaved his head to save time on shampooing and combing. He was the Cheaper by the Dozen King of Robots but could not hold a job because, well you know, working with other people. . . .

———————

We slid the table down the stairs and wedged it into a borrowed van [he didn't drive, though was working on a robot car] and then in his back door, but could get no further than the hallway. That old house had tiny Manny Rivers–like twists up narrow staircases. History bends, but not tables like that.

"I'm not taking it back," I said. Told him he could set it up in the street and sell Kool-Aid if he wanted, but it was his problem now. Sweat poured off of both of us. Me at least, for sure. I shouldn't have slept with Holly Wood or gotten involved with the King of Robots, but Manny was doing me a solid and I didn't want to stick him with the table—him, or whoever was moving into the cursed second floor between me and the Russians. I never had sex with anyone on that table. Too sturdy. No give.

I'm reading my story off of a small sheet of paper. This part is blurry.

———————

Harry was the kind of guy who could set up shop in a hallway. Or sell crack in the vacant parking lot of a boarded-up school, which was part of his destiny. Once as an experiment he tried to see how many days he could go without sleep—he got to five, more than most of us could—because he himself was part robot.

———————

I helped Holly move out of her half of the house the next year when she got a job at the CBS affiliate in Jacksonville, Florida. She took no bed or heavy table, but an incredible amount of cosmetics and old newspapers and *TV Guide*s with her name in them.

She was a hoarder of newspapers, and I was a hoarder of one small folded sheet of paper that took up too much room for too many years. When did I finally get rid of it? Did I make up some lie about that yet, or is that something I still have to do?

———————

Harry was also the kind of guy who could kill somebody, which he also went on to do. He and Holly were negotiating over money—what was the house worth? What would half a house be worth if it meant semi-sharing it with Harry?

We had a lot in common, the three of us. They'd met Claire during one of her two visits to Pittsburgh, so they knew the table source, the trouble/ the trouble, the table. My arms and shoulders hurt for days after moving it. My left shoulder still hurts if I sleep on it wrong or pass a U-Haul on the street. Or perhaps it's my enlarged heart. Harry tried to joke about whether Claire came with the table. He was destined to live alone.

If you want me to walk through all the details of moving the table into his place and then moving Holly out the next year, you'll have to find another tour guide, and, this far in, I can't guarantee you'll find one to get you out with your dignity intact.

And that, my friend, is what the perp walk is all about—keeping dignity intact. Impossible, but some of us fail better than others.

I watched Holly's perp from the driver's side of her U-Haul. [Powder Puff/Powder Puff/Powder Puff.] I was her Oscar-like wingman.

On the road, Holly told me about getting dressed in Jim Morrison's hotel room after he'd invited another girl into bed with them. It seems there was no shortage of LA Women for ol' Jim, and Holly didn't want to be part of an overlapping threesome. How many times had she told this story, how many different ways? Who all got this particular part of the story? Did you have to drive her U-Haul all the way to Florida to get the truth? Harry surely knew, right? When I saw she was a consultant on *The Doors* movie, I had to consult my sanity once again.

Are you still with me? I'm trying to wrap this thing up—Holly's two perp walks:

Slipping into her panties and lime miniskirt, grabbing her stiletto heels, trying not to cry. The other girl already naked in bed with the

Lizard King. Holly already an afterthought even as she lunges for the door. It takes forever to unlock. Special Lizard-King dead bolts—getting in and getting out, both impossible. *Get the fuck out of here already!* And she's finally released to the hallway where, from an open door, someone hoots as she passes. Trying not to cry, but she's melting into a mascara monster. [Too many tears smearing this story, though perp walks and tears go together like sugar and cavities. Right? At least there's no rainy night, right? At least I didn't threaten to kill myself.]

Holly can't wait for the elevator. No idea what floor she's on. Just out of high school. She stumbles down the stairs in her bare feet. Past endless emergency exit sighs. Signs.

I wonder how many people she told/at this point in the story/right when you think it might be over/that she went back to him for more. Holly Wood/TV News/Live/reporting from a U-Haul in North Georgia. Back to you [me] in the studio.

———————

Though I no longer have a use for formal confession, I do feel the need to nark on myself here. For a long time, I used Claire as the fall guy/gal in this story, but the truth is that I have signed many more leases in my life that I have not paid off, and the ones I did pay off were for fool's gold. For example, I sold my Plymouth Satellite for cocaine, and not a lot of it [did I tell that story already?].

Claire moving with me to Pittsburgh, where she knew no one and had no job, rather than staying in Detroit to at least pretend to finish school so her father would still send her money for a couple of more years? Stupid. I wasn't worth it, it pains me to admit—sometimes the less-fucked-up option may be the best option, as fucked up as it is.

———————

A little late, like that drive to California, but Jesus has just entered the building. Jesus got Claire sober. Jesus, man, that dude is supposed to forgive everything if you spill the beans. But he knows you already did it—whatever dirty deed you profess to confess. Repent! Repent! See, I don't understand that deal. It assumes we all have time for repenting, both repenting and living life at the same time. Isn't moving forward a kind of repenting, the hardest kind? Also, why didn't Jesus have more choices? Like, if he was the son of God [capital S on son too?] why didn't Old Dad say, you can either die in order to save humanity, or _____? There was no _____. Unless I read it wrong—I did some skimming while reading the Holy Book, I confess. Was there a less fucked-up option? Am I suddenly swearing too much? Father Frank, who wouldn't marry us, got busted for giving extra-celestial counseling to some altar boys. Fuck you too, Father You-Know-What-To-Do.

[Here's a good one. I cut out the pages in the fancy prayer book I got for my first communion to make a drug stash. How about that for hutzpah? Jesus would sure give me shit about that one, come time for the reckoning.]

What I'm getting at is, if Jesus didn't come down to earth and sacrifice himself for Man [not Woman—no God-the-Mother in Christianity—and even an asshole like me sees a problem with that]—what would he be doing instead?

You can live your whole life in parentheses, is what I'm saying. [Or brackets.] Or—

––––––––––

Surreal sunset—clouds breaking up into orange glow and red stones across the lower ridge of sky. *Nice sunsets here in Pittsburgh,* Betty [current (and forever?) wife] said, *We miss so many of them. We should pay more attention.* Then she went back into her office [a lawyer, can you believe it?]. Dinner smells lush with comfort through the swinging door. I'm making a frittata!

I've stayed with her all these years because she says wise things like that and touches my arm gently with love hoodoo, not just sex hoodoo or sax hoodoo. I'm not sure why she stays with me, but if she ever leaves, I'm going to call you up in the middle of the night and [okay, here it goes] say *I'm going to kill myself.*

Some nights, when I can't sleep *just because*, I get out of bed and sit out on our little porch in a neighborhood in Pittsburgh once lit up by the flames of steel mills, and I smell that burning chemical smell of either furniture stripper or a TV blowing up [new TVs don't explode like that—they just stop working]. [I like a little smoke and stench to accompany my disasters—I'm old-fashioned that way.] Feeling sorry for myself, stuck between the stupid and predictable. I want to reach for drugs, but *no drugs* is the deal I made. I've sold all my baseball cards—the very good, the fair, even the poor. RIP Oscar. RIP Michigan. Mickey Mantle rookie card. Reggie the-straw-that-stirs-the-drink Jackson rookie card. His smirk the same as my old smirk. The Lizard King smirk. I've never told anyone [till now] that I slept with someone who slept with the Lizard King, and I'm telling you now only as a point of reference. Deference?

Jim Morrison was arrested six times. Despite being a veteran of the perp walk, he still appears a bit abashed in the old news clips of his arrest—like, what did I do?

When you walk out of someone's life forever, at a bus station, at a screen door, at airport security, with the slam of a car door, whether anyone is watching or not, filming or not, it's always a choice of fucked up versus less fucked up. Isn't it?

The air gets sucked out of the air. Maybe some of you were strong enough or mad enough or crazy enough to be able to not turn back. *The/last/fucking/time.* Ain't no parentheses around that. Shame swells your feet. Failure wobbles your knees. I can't predict what happens—tears versus no tears—but what is more horrible than crumbling faces, tremors bringing down buildings not constructed up to code, not hurricane proof, not tornado proof, because none of us are ever constructed up to code?

I wanted to skip Holly's second perp walk—the one witnessed from the front seat of the U-Haul that smelled like unfiltered Luckys and stale pot—after Holly and Harry embraced and let go/embraced/and let go/ until the King of Robots wailed with anguish on Elbow Street in Pittsburgh in a truly inhuman cry I have never heard before or since and Holly ripped out some of—did she really? Yes—some of her beautiful blonde on-the-air hair and tossed it at him.

And they'd already been broken up for over a year, technically—Harry was working on an experiment to stop time. They'd talk again because Harry refused to make a deal on the house to ensure that they would. He was wearing his adult shoes for the occasion. Perhaps to help keep him upright. Dignity, that's just a word on a scrap of paper the size of a gum wrapper, the size of a Bazooka-fucking-Joe comic with a tiny fortune/ with a lack of punch line/with Mort, his turtleneck pulled up over his mouth/with a fortune meant for children in their childhood shoes. I want to go back and re-do my good-bye to Claire, knowing what I know. I'll make a paper plane out of that tiny piece of paper and send it airborne, and when she asks, *What's that?* I'll say *nothing*.

I told Holly Wood about Oscar, about the exploding TV, thinking maybe there was some deeper convergent message, given her name—awards, fame, names, fate. I told her all about Claire.

"Sometimes, there's no deeper message," she said. She wanted me to be honest and tell her how many more years before her looks failed and no station would have her.

I put on my adult shoes and lied. Sometimes there's no deeper message.

———————

After Claire finally came to Pittsburgh and got her stuff, seven months after Oscar and I had moved it in, I ordered a bed from one of those mattress warehouses they advertise on TV—miles and miles of them for us to fall on [with Memory Foam and its many knock-offs]. Two guys reeking of pot delivered it, carrying it up the stairs, bending it carefully around corners, while I watched from the landing.

After they left, I took off my clothes and fell down on it in the middle of the floor. I ripped off all the tags, like they tell you not to do. Lying there, skin against mattress, I sighed. It took me months to get around to buying sheets for it, but by then I was used to months of waiting. The King of Waiting. For myself, more than anyone else. I pictured Harry, I pictured Claire, both finally falling asleep, failing to stay up forever. I pictured myself gently taking the receiver out of her hand that night and putting it back in the cradle. Then, turning away, I fell too. I closed my eyes and watched myself, still falling.

Prodigal Son Returns
to Warren, Michigan

ir stings. You get used to it. Were always used to it. Buried it in your lungs at birth in anticipation of today. Dark comfort. Burning oil. Leaking transmission. Exploding antifreeze. A lot can go wrong and already has. That's the darkness. The comfort's buried behind the garage. Cigarette smoke—trying to quit. Lifetime hobby. Like collecting LSD stamps. Marking stale beer kisses on your warped globe. Thumbnail bruise slowly making its way to the top. To be released. Good luck with that bruise on your heart. Life on Eight Mile. Backfire misfire. Deliberate fire. Shotgun arson. That hiss, either air leaking out that globe or a paint can spraying another inscrutable message. Night breaks glass. Day keeps peace. Peace on loan from the bank. Interest on a ticking clock. The bank, a robot hooker. Fire hydrant filled with trick questions and fake water. Air stings. You sting back. The invitation lost in the mail with the lost children. Welcome home, soldier. Have we got a minimum wage job for you! No burned bridges. Our bridge takes you to Canada, that girl you always liked that was too nice for you. Too good.

Ribbons and curls and a mean big brother. Forgot to wipe your shoes on the way out of town—now, you follow your greasy footprints back. What were you thinking, leaving? Like the senile dog, barking at the wrong door to get back in. It happens. Night's different here, spiked with acrid fear. Fists, just lumps in your pockets. Nobody's built a hill yet—uphill and downhill, relative terms. Related by marriage. Separated by birth. Blinded by the lack of light. The absence of an acoustic guitar. The dance of electric shock. One word for gray—hundreds of shades. Comfort, one word for it. Rungs on the ladder: imaginary. Leak in the roof: real. Basement nightmare-flooded. Cocaine cut on a ping pong table. Behind the Eight Ball. Beneath the cue stick hammering down. It's all coming back. Blood on an empty dress burned down the neighborhood, but it's still here. Just needs a jump. Got cables? Gentlemen, start your engines. Air stings with old spit and large betrayal. Rust-mobiles rattling and mumbling their damned prayers. Transportation Specials. Dark comfort dome-light glow. Somebody getting in, getting out. Idling. Flashers on. Adjusting mirrors. Emergency. Waiting for someone. Maybe you.

ACKNOWLEDGMENTS

"Quality of Light," *Burrow Press Review*

"Shell to the Ear," *The Chariton Review*

"Chief," *Fiction Southeast*

"Cutting," *The Gettysburg Review*

"Watching 'Blow Out,'" *The MacGuffin*

"Pop Quiz," *Marco Polo*

"Little Stevie Wonder," *The Mid-American Review*

"Dirty Laundry," *Poet Lore*

"Prodigal Son Returns to Warren, Michigan," *Rattle*